UPGRADED BY THE TRILLEST THUG 2

YONA

Cole Hart
SIGNATURE NOVELS

Upgraded By The Trillest Thug 2

Copyright © 2021 by Yona

All rights reserved.

Published in the United States of America.

Mailing List

To stay up to date on new releases, plus get information on contests, sneak peeks, and more,

Go To The Website Below...

www.colehartsignature.com

JUSTINE

God had to be saying fuck me in the worst way. I thought my crying was done, and after what Blu did to me, I had been able to stay out of his way and been in a hotel room for the past month. It took a lot out of my savings, but it was worth it. My car was now put on the back burner, and searching for a new apartment wasn't going as planned. Today was the seventh day I had been feeling like a truck hit me. My body was sore, my nipples hurt, and every night I would be up bent over the trash can. I just knew that God was trying to sit my ass down before I even really got started. Running to the Walgreens across the street, I went ahead and grabbed two pregnancy test and then went into the dollar store to grab three more. I had read somewhere on social media that the dollar store had the best ones. Going back inside my hotel room, I texted Trish to see how far away she was. And when she replied twenty minutes, I knew I had enough time since I was already dressed. Taking each test out, I followed the instructions and took them one by one.

After washing my hands, I walked back and forth around the room. I knew that if I was having a baby I needed to change. Sex for money would have to go on just until I started showing. The hotel thing would be over, and every day I would do the foot-work to find a place. I had already gotten my landlord to change my locks, and since Blu's schedule didn't change, I would move around him just to stay away from him. Because going to the cops wouldn't help me, especially when he had been on the force for years and was highly favored.

Going back into the bathroom and looking at each test, I dropped to my knees and cried. My ass was having a baby. The thing that was most fucked up was I didn't have a single clue as to who the baby belonged to. If it went my way, it would be Manny's child. Everything with him was perfect to me, and even with it being early in our little situation, I knew he would be the perfect dad since he was the perfect man to me. Tossing all the tests in the trash, I walked outside just as Trish was pulling up. Climbing into her car, she gave me a soft smile and pulled off. The entire ride was silent. A few stores in the mall were having a sale, and she wanted me to go with her since her daughter was busy. So, when we pulled up to a nice ass house, I was confused.

"Girl, come on. Ain't nobody home and I forgot my wallet. It's hot as hell out here and you shouldn't be waiting in the car." Trish shut her car off and climbed out.

Following behind her, I stepped into her home and looked around in awe. When I saw the picture of Manny, her, and her husband on the wall, I smiled. They were a beautiful family and the love they had for each other could be seen in the picture. Trish walked up the spiral stairs while I looked around the house. After a few minutes, she came back down and wrapped her arms around me. We shared a kiss, and she slid her tongue in my mouth.

"Ma, you got my—what the fuck is going on?" Manny yelled.

I put my head down in shame while his mom smiled at him and the Greek god he was with. That man was tall and beyond fine. If I could I climb him and ride his face, I would. Yet, that was a quick thought that left when I looked over at Manny, who had an unreadable expression on his face.

"Manny, stop, you know how ya dad and I get down. I just so happen to like this one a little more than the girls of the past. Y'all wasn't 'pose to meet, so don't tell your dad. His ass a be mad I'm getting some pussy without him." She shrugged and grabbed my hand, but my feet wouldn't move.

Trish looked between Manny and me, and now she wore a frown.

"So, you are doing it like that, Justine?" he asked me, voice so low I barely heard him.

"Justine? Her name is Lisa," his mom replied. Only if she knew, she was making it worse.

"So, you a liar too? Who are you, huh? You got me out here looking like a whole bitch behind you. I was there for you. Whatever you fucking needed, I had you. Let me ask you this, though, Lisa or whoever the hell you want to be. Did you know you was fucking me and my parents?" he asked me calmly while licking his lips.

I guess me not answering told it all, because before anybody could react, his ass was across the kitchen. My ass wasn't slow, so I ran into the bathroom I had found when I first was looking around and locked the door. Sliding down the wall, I cried for not only myself but my unborn child. I knew now that providing for him or her wouldn't be as easy as I thought. I could hear Manny on the other side breathing heavy, like he ran a mile. Being as though I was pregnant, I wouldn't fight him or even go into a screaming contest with him. My ass was not prepared for the storm I knew was brewing on the other side of the door.

"You really gone do me like that. I finally was ready to settle down, and with you. Man, something was telling me stay away from your ass, but I couldn't. For the first time in a while, shit felt right. I was content with sleeping with you at night and always looked forward to talking to your ass throughout the day. Look how that turned out for me. Is Justine your real name? Were you gone tell me what was going on? Please let me know what's up," Manny spoke through the door.

Easing up off the floor and wiping my tears, I felt like I owed him an explanation. Manny made me feel what no one ever has, and I was kind of fucked up for messing that up. Opening the bathroom door, I stepped right into his hand. He grabbed me by the neck and held me against the wall.

"Emmanuel, please let me go." I struggled to get out of his hold.

"I should fucking kill you, bro. I ain't ever let a bitch play me," he hissed, squeezing tighter.

Where the hell was his mom and Mr. Fine Ass at when I needed them? Clawing at his hands, my eyes began to roll. And he let me go, tossing me to the floor like a rag doll.

"I'm sorry, okay, my life was fucked up and I was just trying to survive. I didn't mean to hurt you. I met you after your parents and I had already done what we did. The money was good and I needed it. I found out who you were to them and I was being selfish, trying to protect myself. The damage is already done and I hope I can fix it," I got out while holding my neck.

"That don't fucking matter. The moment you found out, you should have fucking told me," he snapped, flipping the table that was in the hall. It just missed my head. Jumping up, I got ready to fight him.

"I ain't about to stand here and just let you beat my ass. Yeah, what I did was fucked up, but I'm not gone let you physically hurt me," I told him, and he stormed over to me.

"Bitch, on my momma, the way I'm feeling, you don't want these problems," he growled, and I swung, knocking him in the mouth. I kept on swinging, letting out all the pain from everyone who had hurt me. I punched him for what Blu did to me and for what he himself said to me.

At first Manny wasn't swinging back, but one good hit to the mouth had him slapping fire from my ass. I fell into the wall and before I could get my footing right, he snatched me up by my hair and placed his gun to the side of my head.

"Manny, you better not." Trish's ass finally decided to step in.

"Why somebody just was shooting at me?" I knew her voice from anywhere, it was Denver.

Tall and sexy's head snapped to her, and the look on his face went from amusement to like he was about to kill us all.

"Justine, what the fuck? Bitch, I been looking for you everywhere. Manny, what are you doing?" Denver tried to get to me but was held back.

He ignored her and continued with me. "Give me one reason why I shouldn't kill you," he said, close enough to kiss me.

"Because I'm pregnant," I cried. Trish sucked in a breath, and he dropped the gun to his side and walked off. Denver looked at me, confused, and I ran out the door. I stopped in my tracks as a group of masked men started up the steps. Turning around to run back in the house, the next words that were said had me looking over my shoulder, hand on the doorknob, frozen.

"You led me right to them." Blu smirked with a deranged look on his face.

❧ 2 ❧

DENVER

Looking in the face of Justine had me feeling multiple emotions at once. I was happy that she wasn't out here on the streets doing bad, yet at the same time, I was mad as hell about the situation. The whole time, I valued my friendship, made sure I kept my word with the bitch, and the shit wasn't mutual. Anger flowed through my veins, yet the hurt I felt was evident on my face. I wanted to throw hands with her but couldn't for three reasons. One, she was pregnant. Two, Zamir was holding onto me, staring at everyone while we waited for someone to speak. And then her ass ran out the door. I guess she was buying herself some time to be able to have an explanation for the shit she did. As soon as my dad opened his mouth, the door came flying open and Justine was screaming some incoherent shit.

Pow, Pow, Pow.

The shots that rang out kept everyone from asking questions and sent us ducking for cover. Before I could react, Zamir had his gun off his hip and was shooting back. Scrambling on the floor, I reached up and pulled Zamir's other gun off his hip. Cocking it back, I crawled to the other side of the counter and blindly let off shots. The way I was feeling inside, I was hoping I shot that bitch Justine in the midst. Did I want to kill her? No, but I was trying to inflict some pain upon her.

"Muthafuckas want to play with me," I heard my dad yell before what sounded like a shotgun being cocked. In that moment, I knew my ass wasn't getting back up. So, I did something that had become foreign to me. I prayed. I asked God to let us all come out unharmed or at least alive. My relationship with God wasn't all that, and I wasn't afraid to admit that most times I only came to him in a time of need, which was why I felt like for the most part, he was not hearing me. I was wishing on multiple stars he heard me this time though.

"Let's go," I heard someone yell.

BOOM BOOM BOOM

My dad was trying to blow a hole in somebody. The sound of gunfire kept going until tires were screeching. Standing up with hands shaking, I looked around. The moment I saw no one was hit, I let out a sigh of relief.

"Anybody want to let me know what the fuck is going on?" my dad screamed, spit flying from his mouth.

The sirens from the cop cars could be heard. Trish quickly snatched the shotgun from his hands and held it in hers. Zamir grabbed his gun back from me and handed them to my dad, and he opened up the cabinets, which one of them was a safe, and placed them in there. When he turned, I saw that his arm was bleeding, but not enough to had been shot.

"Baby, touch your blood and rub your hands together. Zamir, you come touch him too. Y'all both felons and shouldn't be around no shit like this. Someone came to our home; however, these cops be dickheads, so if blood is on your hands, they can't test it to see if you fired a gun," Trish spoke calmly while still holding the shot gun.

While they were busy doing what she instructed, the cops ran inside the house, guns drawn. Screaming for us to put our hands in the air. I did as told because if I had to go to jail or die, it wouldn't be under the circumstances of a mistake or someone being afraid for their life. Trish sat her shotgun down on the table and walked toward the officers.

"Look, somebody came to my home shooting, they didn't say anything, nor could we see them. I am licensed to carry, and that gun is registered to me and this house. I am allowed to shoot back because my life as well as my family's life was in danger. You see how many holes is up in here," she sassed with her hands on her hips.

The officer looked her over and nodded his head. He began to walk around with his partners, taking pictures and notes.

"Do any of you want to make a statement?" one of them asked, and we all had the same answer. None of us was trying to talk to them.

"You okay?" Za asked me as I tapped my hands against my legs, which was something I did when I was nervous.

The angry scowl on my dad's face was scaring the shit out of me. He was staring straight at the wall, biting his lip with a deep frown etched on his face. I had heard plenty of stories about him; however, I was sure I was about to witness just how he really acted once the cops let us free.

"We are going to bring everyone outside. There are medics out there to check on you all, but mainly for the man who's bleeding, and the one who's laid out in your driveway. I suggest you all get cameras in your house, that way it's easier to see what happened," the officer came back over and spoke to Trish.

She quickly pulled her phone from her pockets and did something, while we were all escorted outside. Once I heard the first set of shots, I knew she was playing back footage.

"The camera was shot in the midst of them shooting in here, see. So now that you saw this footage, we free to go? This is a perfect example of self-defense, and I can send this video over to you." Trish smirked at him.

He nodded his head and went over to his partners. After a few hours of a bunch of sitting around, they allowed us back in the house and left. The moment the cops were gone, Maurice went off.

"What the fuck y'all got going on, and who the fuck came shooting at my shit while my muthafucking wife was home? Bitch, you set us up?" My dad walked over to Justine.

"Maurice, you better not touch that damn girl." Trish came to her defense.

"No, I didn't. That was Blu, I been here for a while. I swear to God, I don't know why he would come for y'all. He was somebody I messed with. When I left out, he was standing out there with his peoples, that's why I ran back in," she stuttered.

My dad looked at her before turning back to us. He rubbed his temples a few times before he flipped the whole glass table over, causing me to jump and Manny to step back. Zamir's dumb ass sat on the couch like the shit didn't faze him.

"That's that same damn cop Za punched in the face a while back, and Denver, you said some shit about someone shooting at you. Did you see if they were following you when you came here? Could that be him? If so, why the fuck he gunning for us like that? Fuck we do to him beside Za knocking his ass out?" Manny finally found his voice.

"I don't know, but y'all better get to the bottom of it, because the next muthafucka come shooting at my shit, y'all losing y'all position and I'm gone take y'all shit over, and I'm beating y'all ass," my dad yelled.

"What you mean taking positions? You not giving us nothing to take, and I'm not giving my spot up unless I want to. I worked day and night to be where I'm at, and you think you just gone take it?" Manny snapped.

"Right," I agreed with him.

"Boy, you know better than to try me, and you know exactly what I mean. I'll have your whole camp on my team before you can even make a phone call. And you, baby girl, you better ask around what kind of nigga I am. Don't sleep on me for one second. I'm gone step behind y'all, but y'all need to get y'all affairs under control and learn how to shut the fuck up. Patricia, book us a hotel on your son, and have me a new damn house in a secluded area by the end of the week, and y'all paying for it. I don't give a fuck how y'all do it, but since this y'all shit, we're being reimbursed. Sell this bitch too," he yelled before storming up the steps.

I looked over at Trish, and she just shrugged her shoulders with a smile on her face. I could bet my last dollar her ass wasn't going to disagree with her husband, and as mad as I was, I could only wish for a bond, a marriage, that strong. She ran up them steps behind her man, leaving us four standing there.

"Look, I'm leaving, Manny. You know how to reach me if you want to talk," Justine spoke with sadness in her voice.

"Bitch, fuck you, you snake ass hoe," he spat.

"I second that," I just had to yell out, causing her to suck her teeth and roll her eyes toward the ceiling.

"Mind yo' fucking business and shut yo' ass up. That ain't got shit to do with you. You'll have your turn to get whatever off your chest you need to with her, but now isn't about you. They shit way bigger than the problems you have," Za spoke to me.

This time, I was the one rolling my eyes. Justine walked out the door, slamming it behind her. Since it was the three of us, we all walked down toward the study my dad held. The first thing I did once we were inside was book the hotel like that man upstairs was yelling about.

My mind quickly was on the events that took place today. How could a nigga roll up to my dad's spot and try to take us all out? What kind of beef did this man have, and why? He had me feeling like a bitch, and I didn't take too well with people coming for me, hell, my family too. We had to come up with a plan, and fast. I ain't blame nobody but myself. When we got into this, it was my idea, and now shit was hitting the fan and I had no idea what to do. We had problems before but never to this extent, and it was no way I was gone act like I was the toughest bitch in the city. Yeah, I knew how to bust my gun, yet this situation was a hell of a lot different. Za was sitting stretched across the couch like nothing ever happened, and Manny looked like his whole world was falling apart.

Za grabbed my hand and pulled me into his lap, his arms wrapped tightly around me, causing me to feel safe and like all my problems were gone for a second.

"It's time you really learn how to handle and carry yourself. We gone come up with a plan, but not right now. Stop beating yourself up about it. The shit happened, the nigga gone, but it ain't like he can't be caught. I got you, you know that," he whispered in my ear.

I swear the way his breath tickled my ear, my hot ass had to clench my legs together. Here he was getting me all horny in a time like this. The more I moved around, the more he grew underneath me.

"Book everybody hotels tonight, nobody's going home. Go out there and do it, and tell Mom and Pops we out in twenty minutes. Let me handle my boy right fast." Za spoke with so much authority in his voice that I got my ass up and ain't even debate with him.

He pulled me back to him and kissed my lips, damn near making me melt. I smiled and did what he asked for now. Blu wanted to play and think he would win this war. He had one up for now, but his ass didn't even know he had awakened a whole different side of me that should have been left alone.

❧ 3 ❧

ZAMIR

Watching Denver until she left out the room, I couldn't help but to lick my lips at the sight of her ass. She had the body bitches paid for, with a small pudge that was hidden when she pulled her pants over it. I was already mad when she said someone shot at her but now, I was seeing red at them muthafuckas coming straight to us. Deep down inside, I felt like both shootings were connected. The fact that I had been in jail for so long, I wasn't really sure what they had going on and how much beef they picked up from it. What I did know was I was willing to lay my life down for them just like I knew they would do for me, and together we were gone come out of this on top.

"Bro, I feel like a straight failure right now. Everything around me is crumbling. The moment I feel like shit on track and I'm completely happy, some shit like this happens. I was falling for that bitch, and she was playing in my fucking face the whole time. This bitch fucked my mom and my dad, bro. Plus, she was fucking that nigga that just shot up the crib. Now she pregnant, the child could possibly be mine or my damn sibling. I've done wrong by every girl I fucked with, so this got to be my karma. Then this shooting shit. For some reason, I feel like Blu, or whoever he is, is connected to all this shit, but why? We ain't step on nobody toes, we literally hustled day in and day out. So, since he wants war with me, war is what he gone get," Manny spoke up.

"We gone handle that. Just like I told Denver, everyone in their feelings right now. We need to clear our heads for a second. See if them niggas know where people lay they head, and if so, everyone needs to relocate. That needs to be handled first, and then we may need to look into expanding the team. Just on some shit where we know we will have shooters outside of just us. I get that we got workers, but that's what they do, work. We need niggas on the line ready to bust they guns with us, not just get money. We need to see who's that loyal, up they pay and all. I don't want to come in and overstep you or Denver, that's just some shit I know can help us succeed and survive this shit for as long as the man upstairs sees fit," I expressed to him while passing the weed back and forth.

Manny nodded his head, and I continued on. "As far as old girl, I can't say too much. That's yo' shit, you handle it how you see fit. I'm rocking with you with whatever you decide. Y'all all grown, and if you want her, you got to look past ya dad and mom fucking her. I mean, I probably wouldn't be able to, but that's what's gonna have to happen if that baby yours anyway, or if it's ya sibling. The child ain't have shit to do with the mishaps of y'all."

"Bet. Look, let's get these hotel rooms and be out. Call a meeting for tomorrow morning. I want everybody there by ten, even Denver's late ass. I'd rather be apologizing or doing time than in the dirt." Manny stood up, dapped me up, and walked out.

Once we made sure everybody was ready and had clothes, we all left out and headed to the hotel in our own cars. I arrived before Denver; however, she placed my name on her room and I was able to get a key and go up in the room. I sat down and pulled a bottle of Hennessy out of my book bag. I kept a bottle of this shit in my trunk for emergencies such as this. Denver walked in the room about fifteen minutes later, caking it on the phone. I heard her let who I figured was her weird ass boyfriend know she was at a hotel, before she ended the call and turned her attention to me. I frowned my face up at her as she sat her bag down on the bed.

"Aye, if you were gone do all that, I could have booked my own room. I don't want nobody popping up on me.

"Zamir, quit playing with me, you know I have a man. So, of course, I'm gone tell him my whereabouts," Denver fussed while sitting the clothes down that she must have gone and got from her house.

"Fuck you mean quit playing with you? Let a bitch call my phone, you gone be acting really salty," I replied, turning her shower water on for her. I had half the mind to put that shit on scalding hot, but it wouldn't even bother her because she was always taking extra-hot showers.

"I won't," she replied, and I nodded.

"Cool, you ain't gone have to tell me that no more. This shit just for fun, right," I repeated the words she had said to me before.

Denver sucked her teeth and then climbed in the shower while I went out the bathroom and onto the balcony to smoke. Grabbing the weed and backwoods, I sat down and rolled up. Today was a long day, and shit was only getting started. The main reason for me staying with Denver was to make sure she was good, and to have her ass target practicing tomorrow. Her ass was blindly shooting earlier and could have killed anybody. I sipped straight from the bottle and inhaled my weed to relax. I told everyone to relax tonight but tomorrow, shit was going to have to get done. Manny knew what he was doing, so I would never overstep him. I did have a few extra pointers for him. Like, we needed a bigger team. We had workers, which was good, but we needed people who would be willing to get down and dirty with us, and we knew a few that would. That was something that needed to be used to our advantage.

The door came sliding open, and Denver came walking over to me wrapped in a towel with her weave pinned up and water dripping down her body. Her beauty was pure to me. The way she looked just standing under the moon, no makeup or anything on, made me lick my lips. Even if she didn't have the weave in, she would still look beautiful to me.

"You mad at me?" she asked me, taking the weed from my hand and puffing it.

Instead of answering her, I stood up and walked her over to the balcony. I made her turn around, so my chest was pressed against her back. Denver leaned her head back into my chest. As I kissed on her cheek, we both kept quiet. These were the moments I could look forward to. Even with a war brewing, I felt at peace in the moment.

"Zamir, I love you," Denver said out the clear blue.

Those words were like music to my ears. I couldn't get wrapped up in it, though. In all honesty, I was a little envious for the simple fact that she wasn't mine. I knew Denver well enough to know that with me, she was super comfortable and not afraid to express her feelings. I also knew her well enough to know that she was just in the moment, and tomorrow she would try and put up a small front.

Burying my face in her neck, I inhaled her scent before placing soft kisses on it. The weed and that liquor was finally kicking in, and I was growing hornier by the second. Denver let out a low moan as I licked and sucked on her neck, careful not to leave any marks behind, so I didn't have to hear her bitching in the morning. Her ass must have been horny too, because she tooted her ass against me, making me grow harder.

Denver spun around, stood on her tippy toes, and grabbed me by the front of my shirt, pulling me down for a kiss. Grabbing her ass and giving it a squeeze was something I had to do as we kissed so passionately but nasty. The towel fell from her body and neither one of us bothered to pick it up. Denver leaned back against the rail as I kissed down her body, taking one of her nipples in my mouth while at the same time playing with the other.

"Baby, I want to suck some dick tonight, please. I been craving the taste of him," she whispered. Yeah, my shit was about to bust out my pants.

I stepped back and looked down at Denver, squatting down and licking her lips. My baby took my gun off my hip and sat it on the table. I let out a low groan when she lightly bit my dick through my pants, before she unbuckled my belt and freed my soldier. She licked the precum that was oozing from my dick and without warning, she took me almost whole in her mouth. Of course, she gagged, which made her mouth wetter. This girl had spit dripping down my dick and balls, and it felt so good that I closed my eyes. Grabbing a handful of her weave, I pumped in and out of her mouth.

"Fuck, Denver. Eat that shit up, eat your dick up, baby," I coached her on as she did that little two-hand twist shit. My head fell back, and I had to admit I was loving every minute of it.

Looking down at her, she dropped one hand and began to play with her pussy while using the other to play with my balls. She was moaning with a mouthful of dick, and the sight was one that would forever be stored in my memory.

"Arghh, fuck," I moaned like a bitch as I shot my load down her throat, and this girl kept sucking. Snatching her up by her hair. I kissed her and then lifted her in the air up on my shoulders.

"Zamir, you better not—ohhh my god," Denver moaned when my tongue swiped across her pussy. Sucking her clit in my mouth while stepping out of my pants was a hard task, but I did it.

"Shit, right there, Za," Denver cried out as she grabbed the back of my head and began to grind her pussy into my face. Her shit was dripping wet, and I was trying to drown in the pussy. Denver's legs began to shake. I kept eating her shit like I would never taste it again. Her body got stiff, and she screamed my name like I was about to kill her, before she creamed all over my face. Letting her down, she slapped my chest with a silly smirk on her face. I stroked my dick, which was standing at full attention, and turned her ass around.

"Put one of your legs up there, but keep ya ass leaning over it too," I instructed her, and she quickly did as I said.

Pushing my dick inside of her, I slowly stroked her while holding on to the back of her neck.

"Shittt," Denver moaned, looking back at me over her shoulder.

I gave her long, deep strokes, making sure she got all this dick inside of her. Denver was throwing her ass back and matching my every stroke. Her pussy was so wet, so tight, so warm, this shit was home for me. Biting on my bottom lip, I took her ass to pound town.

"Arghhh, shit, just like that, Zamir. Oh god, don't stop," she screamed as I used my other hand to grip one of those chunky ass cheeks that was slapping against my stomach. I watched as my dick turned white from her cream, and loved it. Her ass was cumming hard.

I kept fucking her, trying to drill in her that she would never find dick like mine, and by the way she was screaming and calling on God, I knew it was working. Denver's legs began to shake, and she reached back, trying to push me away.

"Girl, you better stop running for you fall over this damn balcony. And take this dick, it's yours, right?" I groaned as I continued my punishing on her pussy.

"God, I love him," she hollered, causing me to smack her hard on the ass.

"That ain't what I asked yo' ass. You said this your dick, right?" I said again, reaching my arm around her and grabbing her by the neck, applying light pressure while giving her deep, long strokes.

"Yes, Zamir, it's mine. I'ma kill you if you give it away," she cried as her body shook harder this time.

I sucked and licked on her back as she came so hard her legs buckled. Sliding out of her, I carried her inside of the room, leaving the balcony door open. I tossed her on the bed and climbed on top of her. Since she was laying on her stomach, I made her bend one of her legs and slid back inside of her. I went as deep as I could too. Denver clenched the sheets and threw her ass back at me once I lifted off her a little. She looked back and kissed me since I was so close to her face. While we kissed, I fucked her real nice and slow, feeling my release build. Pulling away from her, I picked up my pace while licking my thumb and sliding it in her ass a little. Denver's body shuddered when I did that, and I knew then her freaky ass liked it. I squeezed her ass with my other hand and began drilling her gushy insides while moving my thumb a little. Denver squeezed her walls, tightening her pussy muscles on me, making it harder for me to hold onto my nut any longer.

"Fuckkkkk," we both said. Denver came once more before I pulled out of her. Just as I started to bust, I shot my load all over her back and ass. Falling on the bed, I caught my breath and looked over to see Denver laying there with her eyes closed. Getting up, I went into the bathroom and cleaned myself up before getting a rag and walking out to do the same to her. I let out a light chuckle when I saw her in the same position, snoring lightly. After cleaning her up, I climbed in the bed with her, pulled her to me, and drifted off to sleep while holding her breast in my hand.

❧ 4 ❧
JUSTINE

Denver had a right to be upset with me. Yet, I still felt like she was taking things too far. It had been a week since I saw her, and since we saw each other, we had been crossing paths a lot and the girl wouldn't look my way. I owed her a lot, mainly an apology. Over the years, her attitude must have grown because she wasn't the girl I used to could piss off and then she forgave me with ease. I would much rather let her have her space and give her a moment to adjust to me being back around before I attempted to apologize to her. Now wasn't a good time for me to be fighting, so it was best that a talk was done at a later time.

"So, you really were fucking my mom and dad?" Manny questioned me. I was so tired of answering this question, and as much as I regretted everything that happened, I couldn't change it. We had just come back from my doctor's appointment, and while this man was cursing me out every day, he came running every time I called.

"Emmanuel, stop asking me about it. I'm sorry, I fucked up. I get it, damn," I snapped back at him.

For the first time in my life, I felt like I fucked up on my part. The look Manny and Denver both gave me let me know I was just as fucked up as my father, if not worse. At least he had just left me. I had known I was hurting them, and I selfishly continued to do so anyway instead of making things right in the beginning and letting him know what was up. I also could have just simply kept in contact with Denver, and maybe, just maybe, I wouldn't be where I am now. Manny sat my food down on the counter, and my stomach growled. He could talk all he wanted, my attention was on the platter filled with salmon bites on yellow rice, mac and cheese, and yams that I had him stop and pick me up from someone who was selling dinners.

"Your greedy ass don't even hear me talking to you. I should knock that shit on the floor," he threatened, and I looked at him like he was crazy.

"Try me, today will be the day I put my fucking hands on you," I warned while taking my food out and preparing to dig in.

I bowed my head and said grace before digging in. I didn't know who made the food, but the smell was amazing and the taste was fucked up. Grabbing the napkin, I quickly spit the food in there and threw it in the trash. Closing the container, I left it there and went and made me a sandwich. Whoever made that shit knew they was wrong, and whoever told them it was good was worse off than them.

"I just don't get why didn't you tell me the truth. Like, now look where we at. My baby might not even be mine. The first chance I get to be a father, the child could possibly be my brother or another nigga's. Why would you want to even place yourself in this position?" he asked me.

I let out a deep sigh before rubbing my temples.

"Manny, gone head and leave, and take that nasty ass food with you too. I'm sick of hearing this shit every time I see you, for real. You text me about the shit and at the same time, still come and rub my stomach, kiss it, and whatever else you want to do. You come to my doctor's appointments because YOU want to. YOU force me to not tell anyone what's going on because YOU so badly want to be in control, and I listen to YOU. I haven't spoken to your father, your mother, yes, I have. But simply because she wants to be in MY child's life as well as YOU do. I know I fucked up. I have to deal with it, not YOU," I yelled at him.

Manny looked at me, turned on his heels, and headed out my apartment, making sure he slammed the door, knocking my pictures down. Instead of picking them up, I sat on the couch and broke down. My tears weren't because he yelled at me or he pressed me about the situation every day. But because I failed at something else in life, and it was only because of me. No one was willing to let me get over it, and I wanted to so bad. I had to play like nothing bothered me, like I was cool, because the last thing any of them was going to be able to do was call me weak. I had let myself show that one too many times, especially at Emmanuel's expense.

Grabbing my laptop, I went and sat on my bed and looked through my emails. The first thing I noticed was the job I had applied for had emailed me back. It was at a daycare. Blu was out of the equation now, not because he wanted to be, but because what he had done crossed the line on so many levels, and Manny and his mother gave me just enough money to get buy. I had a nice little penny saved as well. What made me want to do things right was the life growing inside of me, and if I didn't know how to love anybody, I wanted to love my child and be the best mother I could be. Which meant I needed to get my financial affairs in order, and fast. The moment I had passed my GED test was one of my proudest, but I felt like I had no one to share the moment with. Even when I found out I was pregnant, most people had someone to call and be excited with, not me. Everything life was throwing at me, I was facing it alone. To me, it didn't matter that it was my fault because it didn't hurt any less.

Reading the email, I saw that there was an interview scheduled for the next day at nine. To be honest, I didn't even know if kids were my thing. I was promising myself to walk in there with my head held high, like I knew what I was doing, and do my best once I got the job. A knock on my door caused me to jump. Quickly getting up, I went to the door, looked through the peep hole, and swung the door open. Sucking my teeth, I didn't even bother to move. I was over these damn people and their yelling.

"Listen here, little girl, I'm not my son nor my wife. You know that's not my baby, so we ain't even gone act like it. You swallowed my kids every time, and I wore a condom until it was time to use your throat. I'm not sure what kind of games you're playing, and honestly, I don't take you for that kind, but I never put shit past no female. Now, my wife took a liking to you, and somehow you got my son to do the same damn thing. Who's this Blu guy? I need everything you know about him, and before you have a chance to lie or warn the nigga, I'll have your ass under surveillance until you have that baby, then boom, you'll die while giving birth," Maurice said, striking a nerve.

"Please, just go," I said, trying to hold in what I really felt.

"Answer my muthafucking questions," his voice boomed, making me jump.

"Alright, just come in, but let's be very got damn clear. I'm tired of you and yo' damn lookalike. I ain't asked you for shit for my child, and I don't plan on it. So, let's just let the sole reason behind your pop up just be because you wanted to know about Blu. Well, for starters, his ass used to live right across the hall from me before I moved. However, he hasn't been there—ask your son if you don't believe me. I told his ass, and believe me, your son and wife know my old address by heart. His parents are in jail, and that's all I got for you. Now you can leave." I was really growing impatient with these people.

All they asses walked around here like people were just supposed to do as they said, and it wasn't about to happen. In fact, Emmanuel's ass was getting blocked, and I was going to avoid them as a whole until my child got here. I would give them all a DNA test and go on about my life. They ain't owe me shit, and I didn't owe them anything. Whoever my child's father turned out to be, I wanted nothing more than to be able to co-parent, unless it was Manny. I wanted to restart and try again. I wanted to feel the love he had me feeling before. The way he held me and sexed my body and my mind would forever be unmatched. Just the way he would make sure I was okay and didn't need anything, even still to this day, let me know that he felt more for me than he ever expressed.

"If that man contacts you in any way, let me know." Maurice went to pull money from his pocket, but I stopped him.

"No, thank you, I don't want anything else from you," I told him, and I meant it. Plus, if Manny found out, he would swear I was back to fucking on his daddy.

Maurice shrugged his shoulders, stuffed his money back in his pockets, and walked out. I locked the door behind him and let out a sigh. I cleaned up the mess his son had made, before starting dinner. I looked over on the couch and wished Manny was there. I wanted it to be the way it used to be. Him on the damn game, smoking and talking shit, while I cooked for us. We would clean up together and shower, then fuck until we both fell asleep. Emmanuel would hold me like a baby, and I missed that over everything. Now I was all alone. Turning my pepper steak on low, I went and sat on the couch and flipped through the channels. I closed my eyes for a second and laid my head back, enjoying the peaceful quietness for the first time in a while.

"Fuck, you trying to burn the house down?" I heard Emmanuel yell at me.

Sitting up, I stretched. I didn't even know I fell asleep. One minute I was watching TV, and the next, the TV was watching me. Getting myself together, I went over and checked the food on the stove. For the most part, the rice was only burnt at the bottom. The gravy and steak were perfect, and so was the corn on the cob, since I had only turned it on right before I had turned the steak down. Manny was yelling and ranting, and the only thing running through my mind was why was he here.

"Stop looking at me like that. I came to check on you, and

good thing I fucking did. You are so careless, you need to do better," he scolded me like I was his damn child.

"Boy," was all I could muster to say. He wasn't receiving any more debates or anything from me. I was happy as hell he came back to check on me because I missed his presence; however, I didn't miss him yelling at me.

"If you missed me, that's all you had to say." I smirked and he sucked his teeth. He made both of us a plate before he went storming back out the house, leaving me alone and in my thoughts, again.

5

MANNY

As mad as I was at Justine, I couldn't help but to find myself going to check up on her or pulling up just to make sure she was cool. Even with everything she did, I knew she didn't have anybody in her corner and was pregnant. More than anything I wanted the baby to be mine, I wanted to give that child, or any child, the love I was given as a kid. Each time I saw Justine's face I was reminded of the betrayal. That girl fucked me up so much that I almost shed a tear or two.

Just like any other time, thoughts of her flooded my brain. I wanted that girl in the worst way, but she was no good for me. Pulling up to one of our new offices, I threw my car in park and shut off the engine. Our entire team was meeting up, and it was time to start discussing this shit with Blu. I was sure by now he felt like we weren't going to do shit, but he was sadly mistaken.

Walking inside the office, I had to smile. Denver was doing her thing. The place wasn't huge, but it had different rooms and it was decorated and fully furnished already. I made my way straight to the meeting room and was met with an angry Za, and Denver, whose face matched his. Whatever they were going through was on them, and I wouldn't interfere unless it started to cross over into the business.

"Finally, I been ready to hit the blocks for about an hour now," Za spoke up as we slapped hands.

"Let's get down to business before the team gets here. This way, we know what they need to know and don't. We need to have shit ready and start a plan," I said, looking between the both of them.

"What's some shit you want to do? What steps we gone take? Let a nigga know what's up and I got you," Za said, while Denver remained quiet with her eyes glued to me.

"For starters, I'm gone do what we talked about, and since you weren't there, Denver, I'm going to fill you in. I also need y'all to do y'all separate things. Once we expand our team, we gone separate them into three. So, Denver, I need you to watch the projects. Find you some of them ratchet, fighting bitches that want to make money, and not them conniving, thieving ones. It's some low-key ratchet bitches, them the ones we want. I need them to learn how to cook work and bag that shit up. I also need you to have a group of like two or three of them to do drop offs. I trust that you know how to judge bitches and can get them scared of you if they fuck up or move wrong. Start them off with small shit and switch up the locations each time they do something. Never have them all at the same one, so they don't know who works with us. Have each girl have their own person to do the pickups. Never switch them, so they only can name one person if anything ever goes wrong," I started.

"Okay, do you need me to do anything else? I picked up an extra shift and I need to get to work." She stood up, and it was then I noticed she was in her scrubs.

"Nah, go 'head have a good day," I told her.

Denver threw up the deuces and left out, so it was just me and I left. He watched as she walked out and sucked his teeth. Yeah, she still had the nigga in his feelings.

"Just don't let that shit get in the way of us all being business partners." I felt like I had been saying that shit a whole lot lately, and it was getting on my nerves. They were grown, and I couldn't do shit about what they had going on.

"I ain't, that's her. She swears she can be in control of my dick, whole time she got a dude. I ain't sweating her, I'm trying to get money. We all know who we both belong to. I ain't gone lie, though, I'm not sitting around waiting for her, looking dumb. I get she held a nigga down and definitely upgraded a nigga's life; however, that don't mean I got to sit and watch my bitch love another nigga. Denver got me fucked up, I done shit her way for way too long," Za vented, and I listened because he would do the same for me.

"I can't speak on y'all shit because I want the best for both of y'all. However, in the end, I don't think y'all gone be the ones hurt," I responded, just as the few people we had in our crew came in.

We didn't have a lot of workers, but we had enough to get the job done. From looking at them alone I could separate the ones who were going to level up and the ones who would keep their spots. I wasn't going to up everyone's pay, yet the harder the job they had, the more money they would see. Everyone greeted us before taking a seat around the long table. I waited for everyone to get comfortable before I went around and collected everyone's phones and powered them off, leaving them in a box in the middle of the table to be collected at the end. Call me crazy, but I was taking drastic measures to not end up doing time like my dad had to, especially if I might have a baby on the way.

"Today is not going to be a short one. Some problems have come up, which you all are aware of. And it needs to be handled. We will be adding more people to the team as well as switching some of your positions based off the work we've already seen you put in. Your pay will be based on your job and how you handle it. I don't think I have to further explain that. I will be offering you all a chance to let me and I know what job you want and why you should have it. It will then go back to the work Denver or I have

27

seen you put in, as well as some input from what Za has seen since he's been home. You all know Denver will be stepping down soon and handing her spot back to Za. That still will happen, we just won't tell y'all until we have all our shit right and running smoothly enough that y'all don't even know the switch happened. Anyone have any questions, comments, or concerns so far?" I spoke with authority.

When nobody said anything, we opened the floor for them to explain what jobs they wanted, why, and why they would be good at that job. Some people were being promoted just because they overworked and did shit right without questions. Once we finished, everybody got their phones and headed out. Za and I stayed back and discussed who we thought belonged where. Afterwards, I would run it by Denver and start making changes if she was cool with it. My phone rang as I was walking out the door, and I smiled a little bit. I had given this girl my number a couple days ago, and she was calling me. I could admit that I found her cute. She wasn't beautiful, but she wasn't ugly. What Sydney was to me was the perfect distraction.

"What's good?" I answered as I climbed in my car.

"You tell me, you had my number for how long and ain't use it," she started.

"You right, you at work or some shit, or you free to meet me for lunch?"

Sydney agreed to meet me at a restaurant downtown she wanted to go to. The moment she sent me her location, I headed that way while smoking my weed. The entire car ride I was in tune with the music. When I pulled up, I parked my car, paid for parking, and headed inside the restaurant. I got our table and ordered myself a drink while scanning the menu. A few moments later, Sydney was walking over to the table.

"Hey, how are you?" She came over and hugged me.

"What's good, ma? I'm straight, just came from a business meeting," I replied, looking her over.

She was draped down in designer, but the jeans she had on

hugged her ass, making it look nice and round. She didn't have a ghetto booty or the ones I would usually go for, but it was enough to watch jiggle and grab on. Her shirt was fitted and showed off her little pudge. Overall, I thought she looked good, and her feet were pretty.

"I'm okay, been working a whole lot. The late nights be killing me. On top of that, it's this one guy at my job and he gets on my damn nerves. Like, he knows the shit he does is wrong but for some reason, they won't fire his ass," she expressed.

"What you do for a living?" I asked her.

"I'm a cop, white shirt is what most people call me," she said, and I wanted to get up and go. My luck was seriously the worst. It made me think if she was 'posed to be one of those bitches who set you up, made you fall in love, then locked your black ass up.

"A cop?" I repeated, and she nodded her head.

"Look, I'm a regular person I just wear a uniform that protects my people. I take my job serious, but I also grew up in the hood, so I know people have to do what they have to do to survive. I don't go around locking people up just because I had a bad day. When I swore in it was to serve and protect, not fuck with people. My daddy's name was Flex, and he served the city with the purest shit up until his death a few years ago. I've been a cop since before his demise."

Storing the name of her dad in my head to question my pops about him, I continued on with questions, seeing who she was and what she liked to do.

"Tell me about you, though, what you do for a living, shit like that. I know you probably gone be standoffish 'cause of my job description, but it's cool you will be losing up to me." She smiled.

I was about to answer her, but the waiter came over to take her drink order and our food, once we ordered and she left I started talking.

"My name Manny, and I own part of a funeral home. I'm

about to open up another business I just don't know what I want it to be yet. I come from a two-parent home; I own my house but rarely stay there. I'm a grown ass man, I've been hurt before so I ain't really rushing into shit 'cause the next bitch break my heart, I'm gone kill her and do my time with a smile," I honestly told her. Well, I would kill her, but I wouldn't do any time because they would never find the bitch body or know I did it.

"Damn, that ending sounded too good." She smirked as the waitress placed our food down. We ate silently for a second before continuing our conversation.

If my dad cleared her pops, then a second date may take place because I liked her vibe so far. However, her being a cop kept replaying in my mind. I was hoping I could use that to help out my team as well as get me closer to Blu. As she talked, I smiled at her and nodded my head, but the entire time I was plotting. I was going to use her to my advantage, and she ain't even know it.

✤ 6 ✤

DENVER

"Baby, I work late hours sometimes," I lied to Joseph. The lies flew out without second thought. There was no way I was going to tell him that I be out on the streets cooking up work and counting money, after doing an eight-hour shift on the clock. So instead, I told him I worked doubles and when I didn't, he thought I was out with my brother or my parents. I didn't know why, all of a sudden, he was pressing me about where I been and why I'm always out late, but I didn't like it. We never had this problem, and it shouldn't start now.

"I understand that, but I need you to make some time for me. My parents have been requesting that they see you for some time now, which is why I invited them over here today. They should be here at any minute now. Baby, just like I put you first, I want to feel like you are putting me first. You have been promising me for a while that you would go to church with us and get to know God. You still have yet to do that. I know that toy you keep in your nightstand can hold you off for a little while longer. And I was thinking, could Raquel be your maid of honor at our wedding?" he asked.

I knew exactly what his parents wanted. I was going to make sure I had it for their asses too. The streets were slowly but surely changing my mentality toward people. I was gone make my money by any means.

"What? That's your friend, not mine," I shouted, looking at him like he was stupid. Everything else he said made me upset, but didn't really move me. My family should have been called to come and witness this moment too. However, it didn't matter because I didn't plan on marrying him.

Wasn't no way that girl was about to be in any wedding of mine. I didn't know the bitch and really didn't care to. I had half a mind to tell him to dress her ass up in a suit and have her as one of the groomsmen, but I didn't. In my mind, I didn't even want to be married no more, not if it came with rules I had to follow. My man needed to lead me, and Joseph just wasn't the leading type.

"Baby, come on. Work with me here." He sighed, frustrated.

"Work with you? Nigga, I am working with you." I slammed the knife down on the counter and looked at him.

Here I was, cutting up fucking fruit and sandwiches for him, while we waited for his parents and his bestie to arrive. I would rather be cutting coke, but here I was pretending when I knew damn well my heart wasn't here. However, I stayed because I needed to come out of my comfort zone, and Joseph did that for me. With Zamir, on the other hand, I felt comfortable, free, and protected. In my man's house and in my own, I was the protection. The doorbell rang and Joseph quickly replaced the frown on his face for a smile. The three stooges walked in looking as fresh as they could in their Sunday's best while I was in the kitchen with a body con dress and heels. Raquel frowned at my attire, but she knew a bad bitch when she saw one.

"Hey." I smiled.

Walking around the center island, I gave his parents a hug and the bitch a wave. One thing about me was, I wanted what was mine to myself, even if I didn't really want the nigga; it was the principle. Nobody could take what was mine from me. She'd have Joseph whenever I handed him over. Joseph's mom complimented me before asking could we speak in private. After telling her yes, we walked down the hall and into the spare bedroom where she closed and locked the door.

"I need more of whatever that was you gave me. I have about a grand all together from my friends and me. The church loves this stuff, Lord forgive me for I shall sin." She put her hands in the air.

She was one of the people that had me not having a religion and just believing in God. They spoke on doing right and judged everyone and everything, yet be doing all kinds of shit.

"Okay, I don't have it on me now. I can have some dropped off though. You have the money on you?" I questioned, and she pulled out ten crisp hundred-dollar bills.

I sent Manny a text, telling him in code I needed him to come with the work. I knew if he didn't text back his ass would pull up. We walked back down the hall, smiling like we were the best of friends. Raquel was standing next to Joseph, hand on his shoulder, laughing loudly at something. Whatever it was couldn't have been that funny, I'm sure of it. You would have thought Raquel's hand was on fire the way Joseph moved it off his shoulder when he saw me approaching them. A few months ago, I probably would have knocked her damn head off her shoulders, but I wasn't on that. As long as he didn't display whatever kind of affection they usually did in front of me, they both were cool. We eventually all went to the table and sat down for whatever discussion they wanted to have.

"Now that we all are here, and to me, these are the only people who matter to share this moment with us. I would like to do this." Joseph stood up and got on one knee, making my wine fly out my mouth. While everyone was clapping and thinking my reaction was one of pure excitement, it was the complete opposite. For one, he said everyone who mattered to share the moment, and none of my people were there, indicating they didn't matter. And for two, I wasn't ready for this. I didn't see him as my husband, especially after Za gave me some of that demon dick.

The doorbell rang at the perfect moment. He didn't even have a chance to pop the question. I was literally saved by the bell. My ass wanted to sprint over to open the door. Instead, I stayed in my seat with my hand over my mouth and wine spilling through it.

"Fuck y'all got going on over here?" I heard Manny yell.

He looked shocked when he saw Joseph down on one knee, and that was to be expected. His ass could have told me he was bringing the devil himself with him. The look on Zamir's face was one of pure hate. His jaw clenched as he stared at me, daring me to say yes to a question I hadn't even been asked yet. He licked his lips then bit his bottom lip, sending chills up my spine. Zamir's mouth opened and closed like he wanted to say something but couldn't get the right words to come out. The angry glare he sent my way had me turning my head and facing reality. The reality I didn't really want. Manny looked between the three of us and scratched his head. I was almost sure his ass was going to make jokes about this.

"Umm, sis, I had brought that gift you requested I get you earlier," Manny said, holding up a gift bag. This dummy really wrapped this shit up in a gift bag.

"Nah, let them finish what they had started. I'm dying to see what was going on and how this shit's about to turn out," Zamir hissed.

Joseph cleared his throat before grabbing my hand and kissing it. He released a breath that he had been holding and went to speak.

"Denver, I've been wanting to do this for some time now. I love you so much that I have to question myself lately," he started. I looked up and locked eyes with Zamir for the rest of his speech.

"Wait, before you say it, Joseph, I love you. I hate being just your best friend. I just think you should know that," Raquel screamed just as that man went to ask the question. If you asked me, that was God's doing. He stopped the question from being asked twice. Using her words to my advantage, I stood my ass up and powerwalked away. I could hear yelling and fussing, but I didn't give a damn what was going on. My mission was to give his mom what she asked for and get to my condo that no one knew about.

"Aye, y'all got some Jerry Springer type shit going on." Manny walked in the room and handed me the bag.

"Good looking, I need you to go give that to Joseph's bald head ass mammy and grab the money. I'm leaving, I don't want to be married, not to him anyway," I quickly said as I grabbed my shoes and purse.

Manny looked at me funny before he did as I asked him to. While everybody continued talking and trying to figure out what was going on, I eased my way quickly and quietly out the back door. I ran as fast as I could around the yard and jumped into my car, pulling off as soon as I started my car. I drove around, just trying to clear my head. I knew before that Zamir was it for me, so when Joseph was ready to pop that question and I locked eyes with Za, the feelings I felt should have been normal. Yet, they weren't. The hurt his face held made me so upset with myself. I never wanted to make him feel or look like that. I loved Zamir more than I was willing to admit and, more importantly, I wanted to make him smile in the worst way. Things with Joseph had to end, I just didn't know how to do it or when. Me using Raquel as an escape goat wasn't going to be the way I ended things either.

It took all of twenty minutes for me to pull into the parking garage and get on the elevator. To my floor, walking down the hall, I placed my key in the door and opened it. I was about to close it, but a familiar voice had me holding the door open and peeking my head out. It was Blu himself walking with an older woman. He was smiling and talking to her.

"Grandma, I'm sure you are hearing things. I brought you

down here so we could be closer. There's no one in this apartment but you. I'll have you a nurse coming soon, and you'll have
some people to talk to besides me," he promised.

I stepped back when he looked up and looked around, as if
he could feel me watching them. When he saw no one, he led
her to the door, which was about three from mine and on the
other side. My day had just gotten a whole lot better, and little
ole lady was about to have a new friend. If I could get close to
her, there was no doubt in my mind I would be able to get the
information on Blu that I needed. I looked back out the door
just as they walked in the door. Closing my door, I went and
plopped on the couch. Today was really bittersweet. While I got
some useful information as well as some new clientele, I was
faced at the end of the day with making a decision. One that
would hurt the man I grew to love, but the other to gain the one
I always loved. The look on Zamir's face was what scared me the
most. I was going to do everything in my power to make sure he
never looked at me like that again, and that our chance together
was still one he wanted to take. Yet, something was telling me
this drug war wasn't about to be the only war I was fighting.

7

ZAMIR

The club was packed, and I had my eye on a little cutie with a nice-sized booty. I was attracted to her in a lot of ways, but the way she was shaking her ass was what held my attention. Denver and I played enough games, and I was going to make sure that I had so many other options I wouldn't have time to miss or think about her. The image of her sitting there while ole boy was on one knee would not leave my mind. Neither would the question of if the bitch dressed in the big ass ruffle dress never said anything, would she have said yes. I wanted to know that answer more than anything, but my ass was avoiding her and the truth.

Licking my lips, I stood up and made my way over to the girl and her group of friends. The closer I got, the more I could see just how pretty she really was. Baby girl was almost stunning, and the way she slowly moved her body to the beat was almost mesmerizing.

"Hey, what you are drinking?" she asked as I stepped into her personal space. I needed to see if her breath stank, and when she talked and I smelt alcohol and hints of mint instead of shit, I knew I could stay around her.

"Why? I came over here to buy y'all whatever y'all drinking," I told her as I waved the bartender over.

"Okay, now let me return the favor." She turned to the bartender and ordered me a triple shot of Henny.

"How you know what I drink?" I questioned her, licking my lips as I stared her over.

"Because I know Henny when I smell it. What's your name?" she asked.

"Zamir, but you can call me Za. What are you getting into after this?" I had to pull her away from her friends and lean in closer so I could hear her.

"I'm going home. You can call me and take me to breakfast or lunch tomorrow." She kissed my cheek and handed me a card with her number on it before walking away. I watched as she put a little twist in her hips. Yeah, I was gone have to sample that pussy.

Turning around, I headed back to my spot and sat the drink down. I wasn't drinking that shit. One thing about me was, if I didn't watch you make it and pick it up myself, I wasn't putting my lips on it. Grabbing my backwood filled with weed from behind my ear, I lit it and inhaled while I watched everyone enjoy themselves. Getting fucked up in the club and not knowing how I got home or what happened wasn't something I liked to do. However, watching other people get like that was funny to me.

"Za, bro, what's good with your fam? I been trying to link with you since you came back home. I got some nice business I can run by you. We can speak on it when you free," said Nitty, a young bull from around the way I used to try and keep in school back in the day before I got sent away.

Exhaling the smoke from my mouth, I nodded my head. Nitty reminded me of myself with his hustle. He loved to get money. The only big difference was he partied more than I ever did. Nitty stayed dripped in designer. He was an only child and his mom worked two jobs to keep him in the best gear. Now that he was older, I saw that he kept up with the brands, and the knot in his pocket and bulge on his waist told me he had cash and a gun on him. He had to have pull, because even I still couldn't get my gun in here, at least not through the front door anyway. However, I knew the people that worked the back door and got my shit in that way.

"Bet, I'm gone get at you tomorrow. What's up with Denver? She still bad as hell," he inquired, and my face balled up. Wasn't no way we were doing any kind of business now.

"Yo' ass still be acting like that over her. Denver bad, but I would never fuck with her off the strength of you. You looked out for me, kept me going to school and shit. When my moms missed my lunch you would give me money, you schooled me on a lot of shit. I just wanted to mess with yo' ass." He laughed.

I was able to hold it for a second before I laughed with him. Instead of waiting for the next day, I told him we could go outside and discuss the shit now. If he was talking anything I liked, then business could get started tomorrow. Nitty agreed, and moments later, we both were walking out the club and to my car. I sat on the hood of my whip so I could be facing the entire parking lot and also able to see who was coming in and out of the club.

"My guys and I be out here on these blocks, and we all sell work inside this Jawn. They ain't afraid to get they hands dirty either. I'm only coming to you because I know you, and what I want to get my hands on, I can't. I owe you my life, bro, especially for the shit you did to help my moms," he told me, looking into my eyes. I could see he was telling the truth.

"That shit with your moms was nothing. Look, I'm gone holla at my peoples, you know I don't work alone, and see what we can do. I'm trusting you to have your team ready and prepared. If anybody fuck up, it's on you, and you gone have to clean that shit up," I told him while puffing on my weed.

He agreed and walked off. In the distance, I noticed the girl from the bar and her friends stumbling out the club. They were across the parking lot, yet that didn't stop me from hearing them yelling and laughing. I watched as they walked my way and looked at me.

"There go Mr. Sexy himself, girl, and from what some of the bitches was saying in the club, back in the day, he was slinging some heavy wood. I bet that shit heavier now that he grown," one of her friends spoke loudly, causing me to chuckle.

If this was the kind of shit she allowed her friends to do, we wouldn't work. 'Cause nobody owned my dick, and I was handing it out to whoever I wanted at the moment. Her friend was cute too, and I knew a dick sucker when I saw one, and that was definitely her. Going to call her, I realized I never even asked her, her name.

"Ayo, what's yo' name?" I asked as they passed me.

"Tasty." She smirked.

"Fuck is that, your stripper name?" I laughed, but she didn't.

"Tasty Angel is my stage name, but Angel is what my momma named me." She laughed, stumbling a bit.

"Well, let me see why they call yo' ass tasty. You riding with me?" I opened my car door and her friend pushed her toward my car. Once I saw her fall on her ass, it was over for me. I wasn't trying to fuck nobody that was that drunk or couldn't handle them themselves. I just felt like as a female, she should have never been out here like that, especially with these kinds of friends. My bitch had to carry herself way better and know when she had too much to drink.

"Get yo' friend up off the ground. You a fucked-up friend too, gone push the bitch, got her ass out and shit. You know she fucked up too and don't even know me, but you willing to push her ass over here, and for what? So you can find out how good the dick really is? You want to suck this big muthafucka, don't you? Too bad I'd never stick dick in no bitch like you, you ain't got no morals, shorty," I snapped, not liking how everybody was giggling and shit like it was funny.

Angel's ass was on the ground, trying to get up with her ass out. Being the man I was, I reached down and pulled her up, helping her fix her dress. I noticed then her head was bleeding a little. On the strength of that alone, I wanted to knock her friends the fuck out. Bitches wasn't shit, wasn't no debating that at this point. I done seen it all and wasn't liking it. It was seeming like I would just have to fuck bitches, because they weren't worth my heart. Pulling my shirt off, I wiped her forehead and helped her lean against my car.

"You know your address? I'm not about to let you leave with these bitches," I said to her.

"Bitches, who you are calling a bitch? I'll have my brother come beat your ass," one of the girls yelled.

I laughed at her, because if she called anybody on me, I was going to see to it that breathing would be the least of their worries. I kissed my teeth and waited for Angel to respond to me. When she mumbled her address, I helped her in the car before getting in myself, leaving her dumb ass friends standing there. We got about three blocks from the club before she got to hiccupping and making that noise people did before they threw up. I quickly pulled over and opened the car door for her just in time for her to throw up all over my clothes and hers. Sighing, I jumped back in the car and headed to my house since it was closer. I pulled into my driveway and helped her out of the car and into the house. Once we were in the house, I kicked my shoes off and carried her to the bathroom. My first mind was to run her some bath water and leave the bitch in the tub, but I didn't want her to drown. Sitting her on the bathroom floor, I ran her some water and tapped her a few times. She was out cold and wasn't budging.

"Fuck I'm 'pose to do?" I called out to no one in particular. After the tub filled up, I picked her up and sat her in the tub with her clothes on, hoping that shit woke her up.

Walking into my room, I pulled my shirt over my head just as I heard the sound of a gun cock. Looking over my shoulder, I spotted Denver standing on my bed with her gun aimed at me.

She had to be the most violent little person I ever met. Walking over to her, I smacked her gun down and gripped her up.

"Fuck is you doing?" I growled in her ear.

"About to kill you and the bitch you brought in here," she threatened.

"You doing a lot for a bitch with a whole ass man that just got on one knee for you." I laughed, going back to taking my clothes off. Denver ain't have it in her to shoot me, so I knew her ass was bluffing.

"Zamir, call me another bitch and watch me pop you in your mouth. Why you got that hoe up in ya house? You planned on fucking her in the bed you fuck me in?" She ignored everything I said.

"If I did, you don't have no say so in that. All that shit went out the window the moment you told that nigga you loved him," I spat before going into the bathroom to shower. Slamming the door shut behind me, I let my mind wander as I showered. I was in there washing my ass for all of ten minutes before I heard yelling. Rinsing the soap off me and wrapping myself in a towel, I ran out the bathroom, almost breaking my neck on the way.

"Bitch, you got me fucked up. You in here soaking wet, looking a damn fool, and all I asked was if you needed something to put on." Denver was seated on my countertop eating an apple while Angel stood near the guestroom door dripping wet.

"Zamir, right? Who's this bitch and why am I here?" Angel yelled.

"God, these people love the bitch word today." Denver sighed.

"Chill out," I spat at Denver, causing Angel to smile.

"Can you get me some clothes please?" Angel asked me, and I nodded my head.

"And put some the fuck on too, in here playing captain save the drunk hoe. Bitch ain't even that cute. You gone make me stab your stupid ass. Zamir, stop playing with me like you don't know what's up." Denver uncrossed her legs.

"Y'all can discuss whatever the fuck y'all want later, but get me some clothes now, for I have to smack this bitch," Angel shouted, and Denver grabbed another apple and threw it across the kitchen, hitting the girl in the face with it.

Angel tried to run up, but I pushed her back. A lump was growing on her forehead while Denver sat there eating the rest of her apple. Angel was screaming a bunch of profanity while trying to make it past me, while Denver giggled at the scene like the shit was funny. Here she was in my house making my guest uncomfortable and doing what she wanted, and, in the morning, she would be answering other niggas' calls like she wasn't just sucking my negative thoughts right out my dick and giving me positive ones.

"Girl, I don't want to fight. So stop, plus, he ain't gone let you hit me no way, and you need to learn how to dip for I go picking for apples again and knock another lump on your head." Denver antagonized her as I pushed Angel back to the guestroom.

"Yo, shut the fuck up. Say one more fucking thing and I'm gone snap in this bitch. You want to come in here and show your ass, 'cause I'm seconds away from telling you about your fucking self in front of this girl. You pull this jealous shit all the time and it ain't cute. Take ya ass in the room and wait for me. I ain't fucking this girl. I was trying to, but her ass was too drunk and her friends weren't shit. You know I wasn't leaving her out there like that." I found myself explaining. Denver looked at me before jumping off the counter and stomping off and up the steps.

"Look, my bad. I ain't mean to be out there acting like that with your girlfriend. I just was trying to figure out where I was. She didn't come off wrong at me, even though if looks could kill I would be dead. I just really want some clothes so I can shower and leave. Hell, at this point, I'll just change and leave," Angel said once I had her calmed down.

"Denver just be tripping sometimes, and she ain't my girl yet. That's my heart, though, we just complicated. Them bitches you were with ain't your friends either. You need some new ones." I laughed just as Denver came in the room with clothes on her arms.

"Aye, here go some clothes. Don't leave, I need to talk to you in the morning, Tasty. Zamir, you got two minutes to get upstairs." Denver walked back out the room.

"Tell her thank you, and go get your girl. I heard about her before, but I ain't backing down from her either." Angel gave me a hug, and I headed upstairs to my room to give Denver the real and exactly what she'd been asking for.

When I got to the bedroom, Denver was laid on the bed like everything was cool. For a second, I stared at her ass that was hanging out the bottom of my shirt, which was rolled up because of her laying down. I couldn't let that distract me, so I looked away before telling her to sit up.

"You can't keep doing that. Shit is really starting to turn me off you. You can't be acting an ass when, rightfully, you still have a man. Until you get rid of him, I'm free to do me." I sighed, taking a seat on the bed.

"I know, and I be trying not to. When he got on his knee, all I could think about was you and why I couldn't marry him or anyone else. Zamir, it's always been you, and I don't want to play these games anymore. I want us to be what we supposed to be, and that's together, living a happy life." She climbed on my lap.

"Prove that shit then," I told her, moving her off of me and laying down with my back to her. If she proved it, then I would give her what she was asking for. Until then, I could do whatever. I wasn't falling for her shit anymore.

❧ 8 ❧

MANNY

"I want that nigga dead, you hear me son? And I want him dead fast. You telling me a nigga can come in yo' parents' crib and start busting and you ain't made a move yet? You ain't got shit on him yet? What the fuck is y'all doing? Either y'all built for this shit or not. I ain't saying move stupid, but at least be doing something. The money gone be there, you can't say the same about your life," my dad yelled in my face.

This was probably the angriest I ever saw him, at least at me. I had to take a step back because he had spit flying everywhere. Here we were sitting in their brand-new house that we split purchasing, and he still wasn't satisfied. I only came to ask him about Sydney's dad and to see if I could do anything with her or if I needed to cut my losses. However, that turned into me being questioned and screamed at. My mom sat on her seat, swinging her feet, looking between us. Usually, she would take up for me or calm my dad down, but today she didn't bother.

"Now that you're done yelling, I can tell you I met this chick. She a cop, white shirt at that. Her daddy's name was Flex and she said he was heavy in the game. I ain't speak on what I do or who my parents were, but I definitely stored that name in my memory," I told him.

"Flex, he died few years back, right? That was my fucking dawg. His daughter ain't no straight cop either. She was helping us with a whole lot. Keep her under your wing. That right there would be a major move for your team." He nodded his head in approval.

Denver came walking through the front door like she owned the place, dressed to kill. This girl swore her life ran on a damn fashion runway. Her weave was down her back and flawless. She had that good leave-out shit too. She had sunglasses on, meanwhile it was raining outside, and heels on her feet. She lifted her shades, sat her purse down, and then kicked off her shoes before she came over and gave everyone hugs and kisses. The yelling I was just getting, she didn't even receive. My dad ain't see her and before she could speak, curse her ass out like he had just done me. Instead, he embraced her like he hadn't seen her in years, and she sat her short ass down.

"So, I have a location on an elderly lady who just so happens to be Blu's granny. Now I want to play it close. The bitch got a few screws missing. I've been watching her. She comes out in the hall sometimes screaming the damn house is on fire. Whole time she be tripping," she said as she crossed her legs and began to roll her weed.

One thing about her was, she was gone smoke her weed and not care who was around. Everyone was quiet while she sealed her wrap and sparked it up.

"So, what are we doing with that info?" Za asked as he walked in and dapped everyone up. He pulled my mom in a hug before going and wrapping his arms around Denver. He kept his hold on her for a minute before he let her go.

"I think that we can watch for a week or two and then we grab her ass and make him come to us. I'm tired of watching my back and my every move," she said with a shrug.

"Hold the fuck up, what place you got that she lives across from or down the hall? You got a whole house, and your neighbors don't live too close, and you barely go to Grandma's house anymore," I said once it dawned on me.

"It's my condo that I use to relax when I don't want to be found or bothered," she said before puffing the weed and passing it.

"Okay, I got this cop bitch I'm fucking with too, and I'm gone use her to my advantage as of right now. Za, what's up with them young bulls you were telling me about? How the meeting with them go? You think we can put them on? I got in contact with a few of my peoples from up North that owe me a favor, and they on standby for whenever we ready to move out." I shared all the information now that everyone was here.

"Why you ain't say all this shit in the beginning when you first walked in? Had me yelling for fucking nothing. Sounds like you do have a damn plan. Well, not too much, but it's better than nothing. What I need from y'all is to tighten up. Denver needs to be in the gun range or something. My fucking child can't shoot, and I ain't with that. So, we need to meet up and do that. We can have daddy-daughter time that way," my dad said.

Twenty minutes later, we were wrapping up our conversation and I was headed out the door to go meet Sydney at her job to get lunch. I didn't drive in my usual car but one I had a smoker rent me just in case someone tried to run my tags. I parked a little down the street. Today had to be my lucky day, because just as I began to lean my seat back, Blu came walking out with a scowl on his face. For his ass to have shot at us, he was moving like he didn't have a care in the world. I'm assuming the guy with him was his partner, because his ass was one of the ones who was with him during the shooting. I knew because I could never forget the faces of people who brought harm my way or my family's way. My eyes stayed trained on them the whole way to their squad car.

When they pulled off, I waited for them to get a little distance before pulling off myself. It was time I started studying his every move. I followed them to a coffee shop and parked my car a few feet from them. They were inside for quite some time before I stepped out of my own car and went in. Walking up to the register, I looked at the menu before ordering me a hazelnut coffee and a breakfast sandwich. Once my things were paid for, I backed up from the register. The moment I turned around, Blu was staring at me. I nodded my head at him with a smile on my face. In return, he gave me the middle finger and a deep scowl.

The lady called my order, and I went over and grabbed it before walking over to his table and taking a seat next to his partner. Blu looked like he wanted to kill me, but he was in uniform and had to remain civil.

"What's good, what you want from me?" I asked him lowly.

"Y'all dead, that's what I want," he replied with the same tone.

Pausing, I opened up my sandwich and took a nice bite, chewing it as fast as I could because the shit was hot yet good as hell.

"That ain't gone happen. You don't even know me or my family, so it's crazy that you're coming for us. I'm coming to you as a man to let you know that shit you pulled was bitch shit. If you had a problem, you should have come and addressed it like a man. Instead, you came on some sneaky bitch shit. Don't think for one second I'm just gone lay down and die. You gone have to kill me, and I think you see already it ain't gone be as easy as you thought it was."

Wrapping my sandwich up, I placed it back in the bag and stood up. Turning to his partner, I tapped him on his shoulder.

"You done let him drag you into this shit, and I can see it in you that you a bitch. Y'all will get the message soon that I'm not to be fucked with. I'm gone catch y'all around, be safe."

I left them sitting there while I walked out. I didn't bother to look over my shoulder because in the moment, thy couldn't do shit to me and get away with it. I sat in my car with it running and the lights off, waiting for them to come back out. When they did, they had to have been on a call, because with the lights on, the sped out of the parking lot. I pulled off in a different direction. I would follow they ass another time. My phone began to ring and looking down, I saw it was Sydney calling me.

"Yo," I answered.

"Hey, how's your day?" she asked me with her raspy but sexy voice.

"It's okay, I just been riding around and shit. My bad about the little lunch shit. I got caught up," I told her as I pulled into Justine's apartment complex. I needed to make sure she was okay since I hadn't heard from her in about two days.

I talked to Sydney until I was walking into Justine's door, and then I told her I would call her back or she could call me once she was off of work. Searching the house for Justine, I grew a little frustrated when I saw she wasn't home. This girl was playing with me. Did I care what she was doing? Somewhat, my concern lied more with the safety and health of that baby though. Going into her room, I pulled off my shirt and jeans and climbed in the bed, where I finished my food, smoked, and went to sleep.

๑๑๏

"I know you fucking lying," I heard as someone shook me out my good ass sleep.

"Fuck is you doing, girl? I'm not bothering you, damn. And where you been?" I questioned Justine as I rubbed the sleep from my eyes.

"I been out minding my got damn business. You can't just be coming in here getting in my bed, Manny. I don't know what you think you're doing, but we can't keep continuing on like this. I love you—well, at least I think I do, and I'm grateful for what you do for me. I also know I fucked up, and bad. I'm not trying to fix it any longer because I see you're not. Don't think I don't know about Sydney, because you be texting her while you here.

I'm okay with you moving on and I've had to already go through the emotions that came with me accepting that. Just please stop doing stuff like this. There's a guestroom if you want to sleep. There is also a couch out in the living room," she said, a little teary eyed.

I knew just by her facial expressions she still cared for me, and I still cared for her deep down inside as well. Yet, forgiving her for what she had done seemed so hard. I trusted her to a certain extent, which was weird to me. For some reason, I felt like I could trust her with my life but not with my heart, and that's what fucked me up. Even with her giving me the space I needed, I often found myself just wanting to still be that protecting person for her that she needed. Standing up, I put my clothes back on before giving her a hug and rubbing her growing belly.

"I only came here 'cause I ain't hear from you. I needed to make sure y'all was cool and didn't need anything. Congrats on the job too, I saw your schedule on the fridge. I'll slide up on you in a few days. Call me if you need anything," I told her before walking out. It didn't matter to me how dirty she did me, because I could never do her the same.

❧ 9 ❧

JUSTINE

My belly was growing, and it seemed like time was flying by fast. I was in the mall shopping for some bigger clothes and saw Denver. Seeing her smile made me miss her so much. Even if she didn't know it, she would always be my little sister. She was walking with a girl who was also pretty. Wanting to put the past behind us and at least be cordial, I made my way over to them. Denver looked over at me with a frown before turning back to the clothing rack she was standing in front of. My first mind told me to try, while my gut was telling me to just leave the situation alone. Of course, I couldn't, and I tapped her on her shoulder. This girl looked at her arm then me, like I had a disease or some shit. I couldn't help but to suck my teeth.

"Denver, look, it don't got to be now, you can pick the time. I just want to sit down and explain myself as well as give you a real apology, as well as listen to how you feel. I do apologize, and as much as I would love to be cool again, I understand if you don't, and I respect it. I just don't want to be walking around and you have ill feelings toward me," I spoke.

"Oh, you don't want that because now you have to see me.

Girl, go the fuck head with the bullshit," she snapped before walking off.

Standing there for a second, I looked after her before I turned and walked off. I went ahead and got me a few things and a bunch of scrubs. It had taken some time to get the job, but I got it. After having to get a bunch of background checks and fingerprints, I finally had a job, a real job. I worked Monday through Friday from seven in the morning until three in the afternoon. I was off on weekends, and that was enough for me. Once I had everything, I headed back to my house. On the way, I stopped at the gas station and got out to pump my gas.

"Hey, can I get fifty on pump four?" I slid my card along with my water I grabbed to the cashier. He swiped my card and handed it back. I made my way back to my car and began pumping my gas. For some odd reason, I felt like somebody was watching me. Looking around twice, I didn't see anyone. This was one of the times I wished I owned a damn gun or didn't have to pump my gas. The pump finally clicked, indicating it was finished. I quickly took it out and climbed in my car, started it, and pulled off. Driving quickly and safely back to my house, I let out a sigh of relief twenty minutes later when I pulled up to my place.

Slowly climbing out of my car, I went and opened my trunk and almost pissed myself when Blu's partner, Tobias, sat up. He had his gun aimed at me and his fingers over his lips as if he was telling me to be quiet. My eyes watered, and I looked around, hoping like hell somebody was outside.

"You better not fucking scream," he whispered harshly.

I nodded my head and backed away from the car. While he tried to hop out, I made the decision to start running. His ass was out and on my heels too fast. I started screaming for help. Running into my building and up the steps, I banged on some-body's door.

"Help, help me, please," I banged and screamed.

Tobias snatched me away from the door by my hair just as

the person opened the door. With his hood on and scrunched tight, he pointed his gun at them before telling them to close their door and mind their fucking business. The lady quickly slammed her door shut and locked it after telling me how sorry she was.

"Bitch, didn't I tell you don't scream? Your dumb ass gone run and scream, right? I got something for you," he said, mushing me in the head with his gun.

"Look, what do you want from me? I'm pregnant, I don't know where Blu is or what he owes you or what y'all have going on. I'm not no good though, I'm no help. He hasn't been by me," I stated honestly.

"Keep walking, and Blu sent me here. I need info on them people whereabouts. Their mom sold that fucking house and Blu driving me crazy looking for them. I need something, and he sent me to you to get it."

His ass was practically dragging me up the steps with his gun in my back. We reached my apartment, and he forced me to open the door. I went stumbling into the couch when he pushed me. My arms immediately went around my small pudge to protect my belly. Tobias closed the door and locked it.

"You ain't gone be able to protect that little bastard baby if you don't get to talking. Where the fuck are they staying?"

"I don't know. I've never been to any of their houses besides the one they sold," I lied.

I didn't give a fuck how they treated me or what I did to them. There was no way I was giving up anything on them. Hell, Emmanuel's address was stored in my head like my social, but I would play dumb until my very last breath. I'd caused that family enough pain, wasn't no way I was causing them any more. Tobias cocked his gun and fear flowed through my veins like my blood. My heart was beating so hard and fast that it felt like my first time getting high.

"I'm gone ask you one more fucking time. Where that man

lay his head? His mother, father, hell, his fine ass sister, somebody," he spat.

Tobias quickly took steps across the floor, placing his gun to my head. My eyes filled with tears that I tried desperately to blink away. I was afraid for my life, yet a man making me drop another tear was the last thing I was trying to do. Quickly raising my knee, I need him in the nuts, and he fell forward, dropping the gun underneath the couch. I ran behind the couch to try and get it, but it was too far. Pulling my phone from my pocket, I dialed Manny's number and prayed he answered.

"Bitch, I'm gone kill you," Tobias growled, grabbing my foot pulling me toward him.

His threats weren't scaring me too much because his gun was still under the couch. The only way he was gone kill me was beating my ass or choking me, and it was no way in hell I was letting him grab me. Rolling over, I tried to get up, but he slapped me, causing me to moan out in pain. Tobias grabbed me by my hair and lifted me off my feet. My scalp was burning so bad, and I was sure he pulled a patch from my shit. Not wanting to go out without a fight, I began swinging and kicking until he dropped me on the floor.

"Why are you doing this to me?" I screamed at him, and he looked at me almost like he was sorry, but that look was quickly wiped from his face.

"I got to," was all he said as he looked around. He slapped me again, causing me to fall another time. This time he was able to get his gun as I jumped up. Instead of charging at him, I backed up.

"Look, I'm sorry," he whispered before he knocked me upside my head with the gun. The first hit sent me stumbling backwards, the second one sent me crashing to the floor.

I laid there with blood dripping down my face, balled up in a fetal position with him standing over me. Manny would come save me like he always did. My baby would be fine because we would get help. That's what I had to keep telling myself to keep my eyes open and listen to Tobias talk on the phone.

"Blu, I can't kill no baby, man. I don't give a damn what you done, you shouldn't have done it. I'm about to leave. Nah, I ain't shoot her, but I beat her head in and she ain't moving, nor do it look like she's breathing," he lied, because my ass was definitely moving around. I kept quiet because if he was willing to let me live, then he could tell whatever lie he wanted to.

When he hung the phone up, he came over and checked my breathing. He sat next to me for a little minute, then he got up and left me there for dead. I knew in that moment if my child and I came out of this okay, I would stay to myself and do right by those in my life. I never wanted to be in a position like this again, and I wouldn't place myself in one.

❧ 10 ❧

DENVER

My daddy had me at the gun range, and I could honestly say this was something I was not good at. Now I could shoot at something standing still and hit it, but I wasn't no damn snipper. I was even worse off if the target was moving, which meant I was no good in a damn shoot out. Each time I tried to focus on my aiming, my damn phone went off.

Looking over my shoulder, I said, "Daddy, just answer it. Don't nobody call me like that but my job and your dang on son, and if it's your son it's probably something important."

"Or Zamir, thinking you with another nigga, and he gone come looking for you soon and flip out until he sees it's me you with," my dad joked.

He grabbed my phone from underneath my bag and answered it. I placed the gun on safety before sitting it down since he had a deep frown on his face and had completely taken off his earphones. He wasn't talking just doing a whole lot of listening and head nodding. He occasionally looked up at me while motioning for me to wrap the shit up. Since it was my personal gun that was registered in my name, I put it back in the case and left the bullets we purchased. Before I could even grab my jean jacket and bag off the chair, my dad was heading out of the room we were in. I picked up my pace and ran out behind him. When I made it out the front door, he was already in the car with it started. I jumped in and he pulled off, tossing my phone back into my lap.

"Dad, what's up?" I asked as he swerved in and out of traffic.

"Justine or Lisa, whoever the damn girl is, called Manny, and some nigga that's linked to Blu was beating her ass. He's on his way but he was a little far out. He was trying to inform you to be careful and watch yourself."

My heart went out to Justine, especially since she was pregnant. I was hoping like hell nothing happened to her. Even with how she did me, I wanted the best for her. At one point she seemed to be all that I had. I was almost regretting not talking to her when I saw her earlier that day. Then her poor little baby, that alone made me want to cry. If I could protect her child, I would. Hell, I would have given my life to protect her child. I didn't want anyone to feel the pain I felt at times or the emptiness I often felt. I wouldn't wish that on my worst enemy.

We pulled up to an apartment complex and climbed out the car. Looking around, I noticed we were in Darby. I was so into my own thoughts I didn't pay attention to where he was driving to. Rushing out the car, we ran up the steps and to her apartment. When my dad opened the door, my heart dropped at the sight of Justine. Her face was swollen and bleeding from I don't know where. Emmanuel was helping her off the ground when I decided to walk over.

"Is she okay? What happened?" I questioned.

"Bro, I'll tell you what I heard once we get her to the hospital. I need to make sure my baby cool," he expressed.

Manny carried her out the door and to his car while I followed closely behind him. He'd never openly claimed her child, even though we all knew he wanted that baby to be his. I honestly didn't see me and Justine as friends at the moment, but I wanted her to be okay. The look on my brother's face was one of murder, and Zamir's facial expression matched his perfectly at the moment. The drive to the hospital felt longer than I wanted it to, and when we finally made it everyone rushed out to get her inside. The nurses saw us running in and immediately jumped up and came over to us. Manny explained that she was pregnant and didn't know what else was wrong with her. I listened to him tell them that she pocket dialed him and he heard her screaming and came to her rescue. He wasn't asked anything else; however, I knew the damn cops would be coming soon to ask him questions too.

We sat in the waiting room quiet as hell, all in our own thoughts. The more I sat quiet, the more I tried to understand what the hell was going on and if this was linked to Blu. My gut told me it was, but why, was the question. I knew that he was linked to the people who killed my child, but I wanted nothing to do with them. I never showed up to their trials, I didn't ask or anything. They were in jail, and that was all I cared about. So, for him to be coming after us like we did something to him or owed him anything was beyond confusing to me.

The doctors were taking too long to come out for me, so I got up and left. Someone could fill me in later. Hospitals and everyone sitting around looking sad did something to my mental. Jumping in my car, I drove as fast as I could to Zamir's house. His house was closer than mine and one I felt safe in. Using my key to enter, I almost walked back out, but I went in when I saw a girl laid on the couch butt ass naked flipping through channels. She had headphones in and was popping her gum and talking to someone on the phone. She was all laughs and giggles. For a second, I listened to her brag about the way Za did her body. A feeling I was all too familiar with. My heart was in my throat, and all the words I wanted to say were stuck underneath it. This girl was laid out comfortable on the couch I bought him, in the house I decorated. The tears that threatened to fall from my eyes spoke on exactly how I felt at the moment. I knew I acted confused and strung him along, as he would call it, but he knew he had my heart, and I was sure I let him know that. Why was he doing this to me? I allowed this man to have my body any way he wanted, and that was clearly not enough. Just seeing her so comfortable did something to my spirit. Turning on my heels, I walked back out the door, making sure I slammed it so the girl on the couch could hear me.

Getting back inside my car, I sat there not knowing what to do or where to go. I drove all the way to the other side of town to Joseph's house so I could break things off with him the right way. The entire ride, I listened to music that kept me dancing in my seat. When I pulled up in his driveway, I parked my car and used the key I had to let myself in. I walked inside and just like I expected, Joseph was sitting on the couch playing the game. Taking his key off my key ring, I tossed it on the counter.

"Joseph, I can't do this with you. I love you, but I'm not in love with you. I know that sounds like the typical break-up speech, but it is what it is. We can remain friends if you want, but I'm not the person for you," I told him honestly.

"Oh, he knows," a girl came out of the bathroom with his shirt on saying. I was sure I saw her before at his parents' church. Joseph's mouth dropped, and I held my hand up to stop him from saying anything.

"Well, this explains why you stopped blowing my phone up. Look, girl, you don't got to be smart, I'm happy for him. I don't know why you're coming out here like that, because you ain't get no dick." I laughed at her.

"Denver, don't think I don't know about the things you've been up to. You left your drugs in my home, my father told me," he stood up and yelled.

"No, that was ya crackhead ass mammy. I don't do drugs, ya mother and father do. But that's not my story to tell."

Joseph charged toward me, grabbed me by the collar of my shirt, and lifted me off my feet. This man was about to see the side of me he ain't never seen, so I punched his ass dead in the mouth. This man dropped me so fast. He had a lot of things fucked up, and running up on me was his biggest fuck up today. I may not be able to shoot a gun, but I could throw hands all day long with the best of them. Grabbing him by the shirt, I continuously threw upper cut after upper cut.

"You better be lucky I ain't call my brother to come fuck you up, bitch," I screamed between each hit. Just like I expected, his stupid ass tried blocking my hits by putting his arms up. When I felt like I had enough, I stopped swinging on him and backed up.

"Listen, I came here to be on some peaceful shit, but baby, you have shit wrong. Don't you ever put your damn hands on me. I ain't one of them girls whose gone allowed it. Now since you a man and want to touch me, I can call my brother for you and whip her ass since she yo' bitch now." I pointed to the girl who was slowly backing her ass up into the room.

"Call your brother? For what? I'll have the police here so fast and have him behind bars," Joseph threatened, and I nodded before giving him the finger while leaving out. I drove the short distance to my condo. On my way into the house, this crazy bitch came running down the hall butt ass naked.

"The house is on fire. It's burning down, help," she screamed as she ran down the hall.

"Hey, hey. Calm down. The house isn't on fire, look. It's okay," I spoke as calm as I could while grabbing her arm.

This lady was in full-blown tears. I spun her around and had her face her home. "Look, it's no smoke or anything. The place isn't on fire," I said again. I slowly walked her to her door, and she tried to run again when we got close. However, I kept telling her calmly that nothing was on fire, like she was a child. I got her inside her house and helped her open the pill bottle that sat on the counter and looked full. Once she had one of her pills and a water, she took it and I left out. I knew I could play off the lady just because of how she acted. Yet I would never want anyone to do that to my grandma if she was still here. Walking into my place, I went over to my granny's picture and touched it. I sat on the floor in front of Granny and my Kotah girl's picture and hung my head.

"I know you got me from up there, both of y'all. Please keep me grounded and going in the right direction," I spoke as if they could hear me.

I never spoke on them with anyone, but I did talk to them often and let them know just how much I loved and missed them. I felt like, once again, my life was falling apart. The only difference was this time the system didn't have no say, so I was able to be in full control of the outcome.

BLU

Tobias was starting to get on my last damn nerve. He was so worried about them killing him and not me. I gave him one simple task, and that was to stomp that baby from that bitch's stomach. At first, I loved her so much that I wanted a child with her, which was why I did what I did to her. I instantly regretted it when I saw the way she looked at Manny and acted toward him. At first my mission wasn't him; it was just his sister. She was the reason for a lot of pain and trouble in my life. I wanted her dead, and for more reasons than I cared to explain. Tobias was making my job longer and harder, and if he didn't do as I wanted, his demise would come way sooner than he thought, which was why I was meeting up with him now.

"Harold, I need to see you in my office right damn now," my boss yelled as I was on my way out the door. Turning around to walk back, I entered his office.

Gerald's fat ass made me close the door and sit down, which was annoying because I needed to get to where I needed to be. If I could kill his fat ass and get away with it, I would. He hated my dad because my father used to be his boss. But when my father was arrested, he took over. A few years later, I became a cop, and he'd been getting on my damn nerves ever since. We sat there staring at each other. He was looking at me with his head cocked to the side, neck rolls on full display, and his top lip curled.

"I'm sure you know why I called you in here. You have yet to make an arrest in the past few months, and most of the calls you've been assigned to, you have not been making it to in the right amount of time. Your car is in one spot, and from GPS I can locate that you are close enough to get to these calls within minutes. However, it is taking you longer to get there. It's also been brought to my attention that the case I assigned you has yet to be worked on. I don't see any up-to-date notes. Would you like to enlighten me on what's going on? Or, if you need me to remove you from the case and hand it over to someone I know will be willing to do what needs to be done," he spoke, voice laced with venom.

"No, you don't have to drop me from the case. However, I do ask for more time. These drug dealers you have me following are pretty much clean. They have yet to give me a reason to ask for a warrant to search any of their homes or businesses. That's why I haven't come to you with that. With no reason at all, I would bring a lot of trouble our way." I lowered my voice when talking to him, even though I really wanted to match his tone.

"Granted, if I don't have something in the next few weeks, you're off the case." He dismissed me.

Standing up, I went storming out the room and ran right into Sydney's dumb ass. I couldn't stand this bitch ever since the day she walked her ass in this office. She was one of Fat Ass's favorites, and the bitch was a dirty cop. She turned even dirtier when her dad was murdered. I was pa-trolling that day too and could have arrested the killer, but I didn't. Wasn't my loss, that man was asking for it. Plus, he sold drugs and I hated them things for what they turned my grandmother into. Years ago, somebody slipped my grandmother something in her drink, and she'd been gone ever since. Thinking of her, I realized that I hadn't been by her in about a week to make sure she had taken her meds. Which more than likely meant she had another episode of her house being on fire or something else.

Walking out the office and to my car, I pulled off my uniform, leaving me in a white T-shirt and some Nike joggers. I switched my shoes to some Nike running shoes before climbing in my whip and heading to meet Tobias' punk ass. I had him meet me at the warehouse my dad once owned that now was abandoned. I honestly didn't keep up with shit my parents owned. It was theirs and their fault they didn't have it. I drove my car inside the opening and parked before getting out.

I popped my Xanax pill and chased it with a shot of Jack. Tobias stood there with his hand on his hips and watched me closely. He looked confused as to why I had my gun trained on him.

"Fuck is you doing, man? I'm helping you and you come here with your gun on me for what? I don't have no problem with them people other than Captain trying to build a case, and you want to do this because I want to back out of helping you. I was cool until you wanted me to kill that girl's baby, knowing I recently just lost my own. I'm not that cold-hearted person you trying to make me out to be. I risk my life for you, and you pull some shit like this? We been partners since we came into the academy, which is why I see no wrong in helping you, but you a selfish bitch. You don't have no reason to go after them people but your parents," he screamed at me like I didn't have my gun aimed in his direction.

"You saying all that to say what? Some shit I already know. I have my gun on you because I feel like I can't trust you. You ready to back out of it for a fucking baby that ain't yours. Ain't nobody gone miss that muthafucka, they ain't even met it. I fucked up and I'm cool with that, but I ain't about to let a baby that's possibly mine and made out of pure hate be here. Fuck her, fuck the child, and if you feel some type of way, fuck you too," I barked at him.

"You are wild for that. You gone get everything you deserve, so if you gone kill me, nigga, kill me. I'm gone die a man," he shouted.

I let out a deep breath, closed my eyes, and squeezed the trigger. *Click, click.* Opening my eyes and seeing nothing happened, I looked at the gun. This shit jammed when I needed it most. I looked at Tobias, who shook his head at me, and I knew then I created another enemy.

"You really tried to kill me. I hope them niggas kill yo' ass. I'm not even gone stand here and act like I'm a killer, but if I had a gun, I would have killed you for sure. Because in this moment, you showed me that from here on, it's me or you, and I'm choosing me." He walked past me, bumping me hard.

"I'm going to tell Captain about that man you killed when you were drunk," I shouted at him.

Tobias turned around and laughed. "Tell him, go ahead. I had the right to defend myself because just like you just did, he charged at me with a knife. I hit him and he fell, hitting his head, and died. That's not really my fault. However, if I went to Captain with this shit you are doing, you'll be out of a job and in jail while I'll just lose my job. Don't fucking push me," he warned, then headed out, leaving me standing there looking stupid.

Throwing the gun down on the ground, the stupid shit decided at that point to let out a shot. I got back inside my car and just banged on the steering wheel. Tobias was right. My father was the reason for this shit. He wanted me to be this person, and I really wasn't like this. I wanted to find love, get married, and have kids. No one ever loved me for me, it was always about how I could protect them or provide for them. Most females used me to help them get on their feet and then left me, just like Justine did. I hated the bitch, and she got all the hate that was building up inside of me toward everyone. Deep down inside, I was a good person, but my father made me this way. He always used his power from the police force over my head. I'd gotten away with so much shit because of my dad that I felt like I could do whatever I wanted when I wanted, and my mom always told me one day the power he once held wouldn't help me anymore, and I guess I was now living in those days.

Pulling off, I headed toward my grandmother's place to give her, her medicine. I sometimes purposely didn't give her, her meds. I was hoping she died, for the simple fact my dad would feel like he lost and be defeated. His mother was the only thing he ever acted like he cared about and the only person he didn't treat like shit on the bottom of his shoe. I loved my grandmother, and often times I was reminded that she wasn't her son, and she tried her best to scold him and make him be a better man and father to us, but shit didn't work like that. Those times were the sole reason I would go and make sure she was okay and had what she needed. At one point in time, she was the person who saved me and helped me when my mom was too weak of a bitch to do anything. It seemed the older I got, the more I hated my parents. They once were everything to me, and that was before they got that little baby girl. When she came, my parents changed on me. They took the blame for things I did, and that was why my dad was able to control me from where he was. I went to light my cigarette and dropped the lighter.

Stopping at a red light, I placed my car in park so could I reach down and grab my lighter, but couldn't grab it. I felt around for a few seconds and then grabbed it. I went to sit back up and heard a loud bang. Turning my head, I stared right at a gun pointed out the window of the car next to me. There was another bang, and this time something quickly flew past my head. I felt a little burning sensation at the same time I realized what was happening. Everything was moving slow, and my mind went blank. The first thing I did was duck down and shield my body. After a few seconds, I lifted up and the car was still there. All the tough-guy shit I once portrayed left my body at the feel of me being on the other side of the gun. Stomping on the gas, I damn near cried when my car didn't move.

"Message one, you not as untouchable as you think. Your

time is coming," the guy with a black mask covering his face yelled out the window. The driver sped off, leaving me to figure out why my car wasn't moving. Looking at the dashboard was a quick reminder I had put the car in park. Switching gears, I pulled off. Instead of going straight like them, my ass turned the corner. I broke every law on the drive home. My vision was blurry from the tears that were falling down my face. As soon as I got in my front door, I dropped to my knees and thanked God for allowing me to live another day.

❦ 12 ❦

ZAMIR

The club scene was slowly becoming my thing, and I was slowly but surely finding my way inside there more than usual. Like now, it wasn't even nighttime, yet here I was in a section by myself, not drinking or anything, just chilling. For one, it was easy clientele, and for two, it gave me a moment to just live and not focus on shit else going on in the world. Denver and I hadn't made things official, and she had yet to even handle shit with ole boy from what I knew, which was pissing me off more and more. She had a way of making me feel like a bitch when I was a grown ass man. Giving myself some distance from her was what I needed. We were too old to be playing games. Within the law few weeks, I tried to talk to her but she would ignore me or walk away from me like I did something to her. I wasn't sure what I did, and I wasn't about to chase her around to find out.

Her grandmother's birthday was coming up, and I wanted to do something special for the entire family since I missed it when I was locked up. I had taken a few thousand dollars and paid for someone to set up Granny's backyard as well as a personal chef who would cook some of Granny's favorite meals. I had hired someone to decorate the backyard as well as get her garden together. Everyone was so busy in their own lives and trying not to dwell on things that no one had been by Granny's to keep things up, so I made it my job to. It was the least I could do since she kept me fed most of my life and was always in my corner. I even had gotten Denver a bracelet with her granny and daughter's birth stones on it for charms.

I watched from afar as my little niggas sold their work discreetly while still moving to the beat of the music. This was what I liked, money still being made and people having fun while doing it. We didn't have the purest drugs, but our shit wasn't heavily stepped on either. I was glad we were selling some of everything, and with my young bulls stepping in to help out, we were slowly taking over the streets. While business was expanding, I started to look into things I wanted to do. For one, I couldn't live this life forever, but I was going to enjoy it while I did. Over the last few days, I had been reading online on ways to start your own business. My money wasn't yet tied up, and the easy way was to flip houses or cars. It seemed as if everybody was doing that, so I wasn't leaning toward that way. I wasn't really into cooking, but I could color.

As I looked around the club again, it hit me. I could buy a building and leave it empty outside of tables and chairs. The space could be rented out for baby showers, parties, or whatever else. I wanted to have a kitchen in there somewhere in case you needed my people to cook for you, or you wanted to cook yourself, but that would come with an extra charge. I also would have decorators, clowns, moon bounce rentals, and all kinds of shit you could rent. Money was always in parties, and I wanted to hire some of the best. I would start looking at people's Instagram pages and put word out once I found the building I wanted to use. I would even throw random pop-up shops and let people with small businesses pay for space and sell their shit.

"You okay, baby?" Shan, a girl who worked at the club, asked me.

She broke me out of my thoughts, and I nodded my head as

to say I was good. When I started thinking about money, nothing else in the moment mattered, and just that fast, I forgot I was sitting in the middle of the club with my gun on my lap, deep in my own thoughts. I stood up to leave and Shan grabbed my hand.

"I'm off and been meaning to talk to you. Look, my baby dad been locked up for three years. I just found out he was cheating on me. I've been faithful this whole time—" she started, but I cut her off.

"That's fucked up if what you are saying is true, but what that shit got to do with me? I ain't got no advice for you but for you to do you. You are out here, he ain't, and if he is moving like that, you're the only person who can make a decision on what you should do. I don't get into shit like that," I spoke from the heart.

"That's the point. I'm trying to do you. I always hear about how you put it on bitches, and I wasn't some of what you're giving out." She shrugged, and who was I to tell her no. I ain't ever heard shit about Shan but that she always acted stuck up and ain't want to give nobody the pussy, and here she was throwing it at a nigga. Grabbing her hand, I led her out the club.

We drove to my house, and soon as we got in the door, my dick was out and down her throat. She was sucking my shit so good, yet a nigga was not trying to be moaning like a bitch, so I let my head fall back, eyes closed, as I fucked her face real nasty like. This girl had spit going everywhere. What got me was when she pulled her little toy from her bag and placed it on her clit. She was moaning and sucking dick until I bust down her throat. Shan swallowed my kids and sucked me back to life. Pulling her up by her hair, I quickly slid on a condom and bent her ass over the couch. Spreading her ass cheeks, I rubbed my dick on her slit before slamming inside of her. Her shit was definitely tight.

"Ahh, I told you I ain't fucked in a while," she said, and I had forgotten all about that.

"My bad," I told her as I lifted my shirt, placing it in my mouth.

I held her arms behind her, keeping her bent over, and started drilling her shit. I was taking all my frustrations out on her pussy. Each time I dug inside of her I went as deep as I could, as hard as I could. Her ass was trying to run but couldn't go nowhere.

"Oh my god, Zamir. Shitttt. I'm cumming, ohhh, you are fucking me so good." She was screaming my name. I let her arms go and she placed them on the floor. I lifted both of her legs, wrapping them around my waist, and kept the beating up until I was sweating. Her pussy was talking to me, and I was liking it. Letting her legs go, I sat down on my chair and let her climb on top of me.

"Ride this dick since you keep running. That shit making me mad." I slapped her ass.

She tried to sit on my shit facing me, but I kindly turned her around. Every time Denver did that shit, she wanted to kiss, and she was the only female I let kiss me. Shan turned around and I quickly picked up her toy that was still vibrating. She took her time sliding down my tool, and I placed her toy right on her clit. This girl's body started to shake, and I had to take it upon myself to bounce her ass up and down.

"Ride this dick, ma, what you doing?" I asked.

Shan started to move her hips, but not to my liking. Saying fuck it, I lifted her from me, laid her on her back, and fucked her until I was about to nut. Right as my shit was about to shoot out, I pulled out of her, ripped the condom off, and jacked my shit. She stuck her tongue out and let me bust all over her face. I was about to put her ass out until my boy called and said he needed me. I ain't keep shit in my spot she could steal, so I left her ass right their sleep on the couch.

"Let me wash my dick right fast and I'm on my way," I told Manny before hanging up on him. I did a light jog to my bathroom, washed my dick and my hands, and left out. I took her ID and wallet with me just in case the bitch tried some shit. When I got in my car, I zoomed off, heading straight toward Manny's house. We didn't live too far apart, and my boy sounded like he was in distress. When I got there, he was coming out of the door looking like he was about to commit a murder.

"Fuck wrong with you?" I asked him.

"Man, I just got this feeling some shit not right. I don't know what, but it's not letting a nigga get no kind of sleep or pussy. I got a chick in there and my dick getting hard, but my mind not there at the moment." He rubbed his head.

"Sound like you need a doctor and not me, nigga. I can't help you with none of that shit," I joked, but I was serious. I just knew I was about to get some more of that good shit, and this nigga called me 'cause his ass worrying about God knows what.

"You always fucking joking. I'm serious, you supposed to be my brother." He sighed.

"I am, that's why my ass here, but you could have told me this over the phone, and I would have told you go to the hospital. I can't do shit for you. Maybe it's not what you're thinking about that's not letting you fuck, but who you're thinking 'bout. Ever since Justine did that shit to you, you been acting like this. Maybe you need to fuck her or attempt to and see if this shit happens." I hopped on top of my car and began rolling my weed.

"Nah, I can't fuck her. We ain't in a good space but we ain't in a bad one either. That would just complicate shit even further. Man, this shit killing me. A nigga gone get blue balls 'round this bitch," he huffed.

"I'm telling you, go fuck that girl one last time or try to, and if this shit doesn't happen, then you know why. She where you belong. People fuck up, bro. It's up to you and nobody else if you willing to forgive what she did. Now I'm not saying old cop bitch in there not good for you, 'cause maybe she is, but right now you have to figure you out. And jumping from chick to chick while you still hurt from the last one ain't gone help you. You might have your wife in there and fuck it up 'cause you not ready or you ain't get the proper closure. On top of that, you got a lot of shit going on to be adding to your plate. That girl in there don't deserve to get hurt because you not sure what you want to do. Be honest with her so she has a choice."

"I be forgetting Denver got your ass on this live journey. You supposed to tell my ass fall in the pussy and see what happens once I'm in it." He laughed.

"Man, fuck your sister right now. We can be on our live journey when she ends things with ole boy. Until then, I'm doing what I want." I shrugged my shoulders.

We smoked until his phone rang. He answered it, and the tone of voice he had when he said hello a few times let me know something wasn't right.

"Yo, Justine? The fuck?" He placed the phone on speaker.

To me it sounded like she was in a fight. Now who the hell would be fighting a pregnant woman? We heard a man's voice and them screaming at one another.

"Somebody wants to die," Manny said as we sped to Justine's house, which was on the other side of town.

❧ 13 ❧

JUSTINE

Since that day took place, Manny had moved me into a new place, which I was not turning down. He also hadn't been there as much, but I knew it was because he had security cameras placed in the house, which were on his phone, so he was more able to see what was going on with me. We kept it cordial between us, and even though I was dying for some of that good loving he put on me, I kept it to myself. My hormones were going wild, yet I refused to have sex with anyone with my child growing inside of me. Plus, Manny made it very clear that he would cause great bodily harm to the person. He had yet to bring up his little girlfriend; however, I knew someone had his attention. Was I completely happy for him yet? No.

My heart was still his, and for some reason, my love for him was growing rapidly. I wasn't crazy and I didn't picture us together or even want to do anything in my power to get us together, yet if he tried, I would jump at the opportunity.

"Justine, where's Dad at this week?" my doctor asked me.

I didn't tell Manny about this appointment because the closer I got to my child entering this world, the closer I got to the possibility of this being someone else's child. In a way, I felt like Manny was only still there because of my child, and I didn't want to continue on like that, which brought me to my question for the doctor.

"He's been working. I have a question about a DNA test. Is it possible I could do one while I was still pregnant, and not harm my baby?"

"Yes, we have a way to do that. With technology advancing so much nowadays we have a few different ways. The first way I won't even bother to tell you since I try not to do it that way with my patients. There is a new noninvasive paternity test. What happens is, DNA is collected from the mother with a simple blood draw, and DNA is collected from the possible father using a cheek swab. Afterward, both samples are then sent to the lab for analysis. The test analyzes free-floating fetal DNA from the mother's plasma and compares it to the mother's own DNA profile. Once the fetus's profile is determined, that profile is then compared to the possible father's and paternity can be determined. You understand?"

"Yes ma'am. So how long would that take?" I asked.

"Results for the prenatal paternity test are generally returned in about one week, once testing has begun. If the man tested is determined not to be the biological father, then the report shows a zero percent probability of paternity. If the man tested is considered to be the biological father, the report shows a ninety-nine percent or greater probability of paternity," she further explained.

"Okay, how can I go about setting that up? The sooner the better," I said as she walked me down the hall for my ultrasound. Today I was finding out what I was having, and I was extremely excited.

"I can have the paperwork put in for you today and you guys just come in when you're ready. Here's where you need to be. Wait here and the tech will come out and get you. Best of luck on your baby, I'll also need to see you in four weeks, so set your appointment up when you leave." She smiled.

I waved her goodbye and told her okay. While I waited for

my name to be called, I scrolled through social media and liked a few people's pictures. It had been a while since I posted on any of my pages, and I would be later after I found out what I was having. There were a few maternity pictures I looked at and wished I was able to do. At this point, I knew I wouldn't even be having a baby shower because I had no one to throw it.

"Justine," the lady called. Standing up and grabbing my bag, I walked over to her.

"Hey, I'm Veronica and I'll be doing your ultrasound. What are we hoping for?" she smiled and politely asked.

"I really don't care too much, I just want a healthy baby. My first born could be either or and I'm going to be equally as happy."

"That's great. Okay, we are going in room two." We walked in the room, and she had me put on a gown. I laid back on the table and shivered a little when she put the gel that she told me would be cold on my belly.

⊗⁍⊗

Letting myself in the house, I plopped down on the couch and waited for Manny to come walking through the door. What I didn't expect was for him to have his girlfriend or whatever she was with him.

"Umm, I called because I wanted to speak with you. It's private and discussing it with only you was my purpose. If you needed me to wait, you could have said that." I frowned my face up.

"I can wait in the car, it's no big deal." The girl raised her hands in the air like she was waving a white flag.

"You called me and said you needed to talk about something important. I was on a date and got up and left, so, of course, I brought her with me. I don't see the problem in that. I'm here, right?" Manny expressed.

"You are here, Emmanuel, but I fucking asked to speak with

you. I told you that, you and only you. I have no problem with you bringing your girlfriend, but the matter at hand isn't one I want to speak on in front of her. On top of that, you bring her into MY home without running it by me," I shouted.

"I paid for this bitch, so I can bring whoever I want in here," he yelled back.

"You right, you did. I didn't ask your ass to, you did it because you fucking wanted to. And you can bring anybody in this bitch, but not while I'm here. Matter of fact, fuck this place and you. I'll burn this bitch down. That's gone be the last god damn time you throw some shit up in my face." I took the key to my old apartment off the key ring and threw the rest of the keys at him. The keys bounced off his chest and hit the floor.

"You wrong, Manny," the girl said as I stormed into the room. I hadn't even finished unpacking my baby's things, but I would leave everything he purchased. I grabbed the bassinet I paid for and began filling it with the clothes and things I brought, and I dragged it to the living room.

"What the hell, Justine, you called me here to help you move?" Trish asked.

"No, but could you please help me?" I asked her, angrily wiping my tears.

"Manny, what the hell you do?" Denver asked, and it felt good for her to be taking up for me again.

"I ain't do shit. She called me here and I brought Sydney. She mad 'cause I had her in here without telling her," he said like nothing was wrong with it.

"So, if I brought my man to your house without telling you then it's cool, right? Because that's what you're standing here saying." I got in his face, pushing him.

"Nah, look, my bad, okay. You don't have to leave here. Your old spot not safe, that's why you here. Come on, we can talk in private," he spoke.

"No, I don't want to. I wanted to ask you could you come

tomorrow and do a DNA test so we can know now," I blurted out.

Emmanuel looked at me like I had lost my damn mind. He wiped his hand over his face before looking at me again. His head turned to the side, and he laughed, and not like a shit was funny laugh.

"What the fuck I told you? Huh? You forgot that's my god damn baby no matter what a test says? I told you we ain't fucking need one 'cause I'm gone be the dad regardless. Ain't I told you that?" he barked, spitting flying out his mouth.

I took a step back, but he only took a step forward to stay in my face. "Ain't that's what the fuck I said?" he repeated himself.

"Yes," I whimpered.

"You need to get out her face." Denver pulled his arm, and he pushed her off of him and punched a hole in my wall.

"Don't fucking touch me, and don't tell me what I need to do. Why you want to know so bad, huh? You want to take my baby from me?" He tried to come back toward me, but this time Denver pushed him back, and he looked at her like he was about to put her on her ass.

"I wish the fuck you would," his mom said.

"I want my son to know who his dad is just in case, Emmanuel. You'll always be his father, but say if something happens and he needs blood and you're not a match. I'm not trying to take him from you," I spoke through tears.

"So, we having a boy? I'm about to have me a son and you want to do this now? You want to fucking break me more than you already did?" Manny yelled at me, on the verge of tears.

"I'm not doing anything to you but wanting to know. I understand everything you saying. I hurt a lot of people and I don't want to do that with my son. I want me and him to have a good relationship. I want him to trust me and know that I always decided to do what was best for him. No matter what or who it hurts, my son is my top priority," I told him, wiping my tears.

"Fuck it, this what you want, then cool. But blood or not, I wish you would let my son call another man dad." Emmanuel walked out.

He had been doing that a lot lately, and us being on the same page was seeming to slip further and further away.

"You gone be good. You did what you did, but my nephew gone be straight. You're not a bad person for wanting to know, and if it helps clear your conscious, fuck what he's talking about." Denver hugged me.

"Thank you, I don't want to hurt him. I've done enough and I know how important this baby is to him. I would never take him from him or not let him be in his life. I want to be able to do this parenting thing with him the right way. I don't know if I can, though, if he's going to keep acting like this. Every time he gets mad, he's punching holes in shit or storming out. My son ain't gone witness that, he gone see love," I said as I got myself together.

Trish took my baby things back in his room before she came and sat down with me. The entire time she talked to me, she was honest and didn't pick sides. She helped me understand Manny's side as well as saying she would explain to him what I was doing was right. I respected her for that. All I wanted was for my son to be happy, that would make me happy. I may have failed everyone around me, but on my soul, I wouldn't fail him.

❧ 14 ❧

DENVER

I was putting my all into work and building my team, so I didn't have time for anything else. I was letting the guys handle the shit with Blu and when it was time for me to step in, I would. Manny's ass was on a rampage trying to find Tobias, who I learned was Blu's partner. This man had to be hiding out at his job because we had been by his house plenty of times. I was just the driver for them because we all knew if I went in shooting, I was gone miss.

"Why are you calling my phone? Hyneef is supposed to stay with you this weekend," Angel hissed in the phone.

Yeah, I had linked up with her to be on my team. I only wanted to deal with females who had shit to lose just like me. So, opening their mouth was a no go if it came down to it, and being caught was something they didn't want, so they were extra cautious. Unlike my brother said, I introduced the girls to each other. I wanted them to know who to expect and what everyone looked like. However, I didn't tell them who was going to be doing what. They would see when the time came. Each of them had their own individual job and I kept them on teams, two girls for each job. Not only were we going to hustle together, but we were going to build together.

"Girl." Bianca laughed like she understood what Angel was going through.

"Look, when she's done, we gone discuss some more shit and then we gone go out to drink." I wanted my girls to feel good and appreciated.

I wanted them to feel like we were all on one accord, and even though I was higher up than them, I wouldn't treat them as such unless they made me. Angel hung her phone up and I began speaking.

"As I was saying, we have to put our trust in one another, build a bond, and make money at the same time." I clapped my hands.

"Yo, sorry to interrupt, but let me holla at you for a second." Zamir came walking into my office.

"I'm handling something right now, so you got to wait," I replied, not bothering to look at him.

His ass needed to be demanding shit from his couch potato and not me. Zamir stood there for a second, looking at me while I continued on what I was saying.

"Denver, quit fucking playing with me and get up. You want me to show my ass up in here in front these females, don't you?" he said, pulling up his gray sweats.

I laughed at him as my eyes immediately went down to that devil, and I licked my lips. He wasn't hard, but the way his print sat there you would have thought he was. I caught a few of them looking, but they could never taste it because it rightfully belonged to me, and Za would not mess with anybody that worked with me. This man just swore up and down I was about to move. He could show his ass all he wanted to, the fact still remained he was slinging dick and it wasn't my way at the moment.

"Watch out, I'm busy. It can wait. I'll hit you up when I'm done." I dismissed him.

Zamir shook his head before he pulled his pants up squatted down to my level and lifted me up. My legs wrapped around his waist, and he placed my back against the wall with one hand on my neck and the other rested next to my head.

"When I speak, you listen. Now what's with your bullshit? You ain't been staying home or at your parents, so where are you laying your head at night? Say another nigga and watch his ass come up fucking missing," he whispered harshly in my ear.

I ain't gone lie, my shit was dripping wet, but that was none of his business. I laughed at him before turning my head. "You mind letting me down? As long as you got bitches up in your crib, Zamir, don't question me. 'Cause you ain't make it your business to let me know who you were sticking dick to, so don't make it yours to find out who could possibly be sliding in my shit," I said with attitude.

This man wrapped both hands around my neck and applied pressure. "Say that shit again." He squeezed tighter. I tried to pry his hands from off of me, but the shit wasn't working. Angel went to help me by grabbing his arm. He let me go with one hand and whipped his gun out and in her face so fast.

"I ain't got no problem with you, but don't fucking touch me. None of y'all told y'all little friend not to make me show my ass, but this what she wanted," he politely said.

"Oh, hell nah, he crazy. But that shit sexy, and look at her ass about to pass out, yet looking like she's having an orgasm. We gone wait in the hall for y'all." Cookie laughed.

Zamir let me go, and once my feet touched the ground, I slapped the shit out of him. He wiped his mouth before stepping back into my personal space. "You know I miss your nut ass and you got me in here tripping. I fucked ole girl one time because you were playing with me. The only reason she was in the crib was 'cause Justine had that shit going on and I was rushing to get by my brother's side." He sat down in the chair.

"You better apologize to Angel. I don't care why you was fucking her. The moment I mention fucking somebody else, you want to choke a bitch out," I replied.

"I might apologize to her. She shouldn't have touched me.

What we got going on is between us. I would never hurt you. I knew yo' hot pussy ass was getting wet off that shit because my stomach was getting warm. You ended shit with ya boy?" he asked me.

"Yeah, I did, and you're going to apologize. Mad or not, that wasn't okay. She was just trying to help me."

"After you hit her in the head with an apple? She crazy. I wanted to ask you to go on a date with me. I want to do shit right with you, and I ain't never been on a date before, like a real date, but I had some special help planning this shit out for you. So, you can't say no." He smirked, pulling me onto his lap.

"Okay, I'll go." I kissed his lips. Zamir slipped his tongue into my mouth and kissed me with so much passion it made me dizzy. His dick hardened underneath me, and I went to get up.

"Nah, fuck that. The door closed and I'm sure locked, lift up. You want to be out here in these little ass shorts, right?" he said, ripping them right in the middle along with my panties. Zamir whipped his dick out and slowly slid me down on him.

"Fuck," I gasped.

"I knew my shit was wet, but not like this. You missed daddy, huh?" he groaned as he guided me up and down at the pace he wanted me to go. Grabbing his hands, I intertwined our fingers and rocked my hips back and forth. Looking down at him with his eyes closed and head leaned back, I had to kiss him. I pecked his lips a few times before licking his bottom one and pulling it into my mouth with my teeth. Zamir moaned out before he lifted me up and laid me back on the table.

This man pulled my heels off and placed my legs against his chest before he leaned forward and began stroking me like he was punishing me.

"Arghhh, you going too deep," I cried out. This man was fucking me so deep it made my stomach hurt.

"Stop bitching." He smacked my hands off of him so I couldn't push him back. He grabbed my foot and sucked on my toes while punishing my kitty.

"Fuckkk, Zamir," I screamed as I came all over him. He picked up his pace, kissing me to muffle out my screams. Seconds later, his body jerked a few times, and he came. This man didn't bother to pull out or anything.

"Yo' ass ain't gone be able to show off in front of your friends no more the way you just were screaming." He laughed.

I smacked his chest before climbing down off the table. We cleaned up our mess and wiped the tables and chairs down with Clorox wipes. I ran into the bathroom and cleaned myself up as best as I could.

"Fuck I'm 'pose to do about my shorts?" I asked him.

"Shit, I don't know. You ain't got no clothes in your car or in here?"

"I think I got some tights in my car. Can you go grab them for me? Tell the girls I'll be out in a second." I tossed him my keys and he left out, closing the door behind him. A few minutes later, he returned with my tights. I pulled them on, and he smacked my ass.

"That muthafucka so juicy. I can't wait to put my face in it. Be ready tonight by nine." He pulled me into him and kissed me deeply before pecking my lips and walking out the room.

"Aye, I love yo' bald headed ass," he called out.

"Aww," the girls cooed, and I gave them the finger.

"Love you too, Za," I responded, blowing him a kiss.

When he left out, everyone started talking. Angel just smirked and left well enough alone. She knew what was up with me and him, and she didn't speak on it. I liked that about her.

"Okay, back to what we were doing before we got interrupted. Umm, basically, you all know one another's drops will never be at the same time, on the same day, or at the same location. No one else can pick up or drop off, just us. Money will be given directly to me, and I'll handle the rest. Each day you do a drop you will be paid once the money is in my hand. I do advise you all to become friends, trust each other, don't back door each other, and support each other because at the end of the day, I want us all to grow and eat good," I explained for the last time.

Once I was sure everyone got it, we all left and went our separate ways. I quickly went home and went straight for my bathroom, bypassing the pile of mail on the floor at my door. I would pick it up once I washed my ass. I turned on the shower and let it warm up while I peeled out of my clothes. Grabbing my rag, I soaped it up with my Dove soap and washed my body twice then rinsed off. Turning the water off, I grabbed my towel and wrapped it around my body. I walked into my room and plopped down on my bed. Grabbing my phone, I skimmed through my text messages and decided I could take a quick nap since it was only three in the afternoon. Laying in my bed, I scrolled through Instagram, until Manny texted me saying meet him at the funeral home. Climbing back out my bed, I slipped on a pair of skinny jeans, some heels, and a cute little shirt. I walked out of the house and made it to my destination in less than twenty minutes. When I walked inside the funeral home, everything was quiet just like it was supposed to be.

"He's in the basement," Dex, our security, let me know.

I took the steps and my mouth dropped when I saw Emmanuel, with his gloves on and Tobias sitting in a chair.

❧ 15 ❧

MANNY

I had been planning this day for the last few weeks. It was time niggas started to feel some type of pain. Enough time had gone past since I sent Blu a message. I told my shooters to miss on purpose. Today I was going to show him that I was not one of those people who let shit go and not do nothing back. It may have taken some time, but shit was going to get done. I was hoping his friend losing his life let him know that I was coming for him. I liked to wait because I wanted him to get comfortable, and then I wanted to make him uncomfortable. I wanted him to live his last days watching over his shoulder and nervous.

"So, Tobias, why you wanted to fuck with me? You could have caused harm to my son. My child who ain't even have a chance to see this cruel ass world yet. Then you put hands on a female, a fucking female, and lastly, you shot at me, my sister, brother, and my dad. Hell, my mom was in that house and you could have killed her. All for what? Your partner. Damn, it sucks he got you in this shit." I laughed as I circled him in the chair.

My thoughts were all over the place. I wanted to just shoot him and get it over with. At the same time, I wanted to torture him and then kill him. My heart was beating fast and for some reason, I was excited, like overly excited. Should I cut his fingers off? Or get on some *State Property* shit and shoot the hand he shot at us with. Then there was the question of just getting the shit over with. Either way, this man was dying by my hands and my hands only.

"Who was them niggas that was shooting at us? It was way more than just two of you," Denver asked him.

"I don't know them, Blu hired them. All this comes down to you and Justine. This is why he is doing this, from my knowledge. Look, I wasn't going to kill the baby, and that's why he just tried to kill me. I lost a child and that was too reckless for me." His voice was cracking, and he must have known just like I knew, today was his last day.

"All that's cool, but what's done is done. Can you come on Mr. Take Ya Time and Kill People? I got some shit to do today, and it doesn't require me sitting here all day," Zamir spoke up.

Laughing at him, I decided I wanted to snatch his fingernails off the hand he pulled the trigger with. I grabbed a pair of tweezers and did just that. The pain from him screaming made me smile while Denver winced. I shot him once in that very same hand and then just said fuck it. I was gone burn his ass alive.

"What part of you do you want me to leave on Blu's doorstep?" I asked Tobias.

"None, just kill me. Shoot me and take me out of this pain, please," he cried as he held his hand to his chest, like that would ease the pain.

"Okay. Tell them open the crematory, his ass going in like this," I told Denver.

"You gone burn this man alive?" Zamir asked with a shocked facial expression.

"Hell yeah," I replied.

Once Denver came back, Zamir and I carried Tobias to the room where we cremated people. His ass was screaming and pleading the whole way. He even fell on the floor a few times, which was why we opted on carrying him. We threw his ass in that hot ass oven and listened to him scream for all of three seconds.

"Ashes to ashes, dust to dust, lord forgive us," I said before walking out.

"You are wild. Now can we all get ready? It's Grandma's birthday and I want to take the family somewhere nice. Meet me at Grandma's by nine. Denver, you already know I'm picking you up, and everyone else is going to meet us there. I just want to release balloons at her house," Zamir told me. He was so adamant about being in charge of what we do for Grandma's birthday, and now he had us all on a damn time schedule.

"I'm bringing Sydney," I told them.

"Okay, Justine will be there, so please don't be doing your wall punching thing." Denver used her fingers to air quote wall punching.

"You just worry about y'all, and y'all almost but not really in a relationship activity. I'm just happy we can carry on with business even when we all know y'all mad at each other."

"Man, we out, see you at nine." Zamir grabbed Denver's hand and pulled her out the place. I, on the other hand, went into our office and sent out payments to staff before heading home.

Sydney was pulling up at the same time as me. I got out my car first then went over and helped her out of her car. She smiled at me, and I smiled back. Today she wasn't in her uniform nor was her hair pulled back in a bun. She had a nice weave that touched the middle of her back. It had a little side bang thing going on and made her look different.

"My family going out for my grandma's birthday. She passed away and we celebrate it every year. I know I been keeping you cooped up in the house under me, but if you want to go with me, you can."

"Are you asking me to go with you? Because I would love to." She pecked my lips.

"Bet, Justine gone be there as well. Just so you know," I told her.

"Okay. That's good. As of now, I don't plan on going anywhere unless you make me. I want to be cool with her since she's the mother of your child. I'll need her to know if you can't do something or you're busy and I'm not, she can call on me. You know I'm not her enemy." When that shit left her lips, I knew then that she was a keeper. Any other girl would have been mad or acted like they had a point to prove.

We walked hand in hand inside the house. Sydney sat on my bed while I ran and took a quick shower. I let my water run while I stripped out of my clothes. I stepped in and let the water help me clear my mind. I washed my hair then my ass and got out. Wrapping my towel around my waist, I went back inside my room.

"Can I at least taste the dick? You been holding out and I'm tired of waiting. Come fuck me," Sydney said. She was on my bed butt ass naked, on her hands and knees. My dick stood at attention and was so hard that shit hurt. She stood up, pulled my towel off of me, and pushed me on the bed. I laid back and this girl climbed on top of me, putting her pussy in my face. Me being me, I smelled it first. I groaned when I felt her warm, wet mouth since I couldn't see what she was doing.

"Mm, daddy, I'm about to suck you dry," she moaned as she latched on to my dick like it was a popsicle on a hot day.

"OH, fuck girl." I slapped her ass.

Saying fuck it, I went in for the kill. I used the tip of my tongue to lick her pussy before lightly sucking on her pearl. Her whole body jerked when I did that, but she never stopped sucking. While I licked and sucked on her clit, I slid two fingers inside her wet tunnel and pumped them, making her moan out loud.

"Mmhmm. Keep sucking," I coached her on, before spitting on her pussy and licking it. I was tearing her shit up too. She started to grind her puss into my face, so I wrapped my arms around her waist, keeping her in one spot. I flicked my tongue against her swollen clit as fast as I could, causing her body to shudder while she came in my mouth. I grunted, shooting my load down her throat.

Sydney rolled off of me and I grabbed a condom from my drawer next to me. Sliding it on my dick, I slapped her ass.

"You wanted to fuck, right?" I smirked, stroking my dick back to life.

She was laying on her right side, so I kneeled down in front of her, straddling her right leg. I lifted her left one and wrapped it around my left side. I used my other hand to guide my dick into her wet tunnel. She gasped at my entrance. I squeezed her leg while I pumped in and out of her. I could have taken my time, but she told me to fuck her. I grabbed her ass cheek and lifted it, squeezing it while I fucked her hard. Her moans were like music to my ears and only caused me to go harder, to make her call me daddy louder. The headboard was knocking against the wall.

"You wanted me to fuck you, right?" I slapped her ass.

"Yes, daddy, right there. Please don't stop," she cried out as I continuously hit her spot. I kept hitting it until her body began to shake and her soft moans turned into loud screams. She squirted all over me, making me pull out and flip her over. She laid on her back and locked her legs at the ankles behind her head. My ass smiled like a kid in the candy store.

"Oh, you really want to scream, huh?" I slapped her thigh and inserted myself, this time more slowly.

I was in the push-up position as I gave her nothing but big dick. I used my thumb to rub her clit while I fucked the shit out of her.

"You going too deep. Fuck, oh my god, you're so big," she screamed while trying to drop her legs.

I held them bitches up. She should have never let me this deep in her in the first place. I was long stroking the pussy and my nut was rising. Her body was shaking again, so I rubbed her clit faster while I pumped faster and harder.

"Ahh, fuck," I let out as I bit into her leg while shooting my load in the condom. Letting her legs go, I stood up and went to flush the condom in the toilet. Her ass followed me, and we took a shower together. For a moment, I just held her in my arms and kissed all over her face and lips.

"I'm fucking you all the time now," I told her as we washed up.

"If it's gone be like you just had me, I want it all the time." She smirked.

"It gets better."

We got out the shower and got dressed then headed over to my grandma's place. We were the first people to arrive. There was a big ass sign with balloons on it that said *wait here*. I knew it was Za's handwriting because he wrote sloppy as hell. Looking at my watch, I noticed we were fifteen minutes early, and fucking around with Denver, they ass wouldn't be on time. Sitting on the step, I pulled my weed out my pocket and began to roll it up. As soon as I lit it, my dad and mom pulled up.

"Hey, son, how are you doing?" my mom spoke to Sydney and me.

"What's up, Ma, you look beautiful. You owe me a dance tonight too. Fuck yo' husband, he old now anyway," I told her as I pulled her into a hug.

"Don't get fucked up," my dad warned.

I introduced everyone just as Za, Denver, and Justine pulled up. Everyone was dressed casually but my extra ass sister, who had on all white with purple heels. This girl could be going to an event where she would stand all night and have heels on.

"I want to release the balloons in the backyard, so let's go this way." Za led the way.

"Oh my god, Zamir, you didn't," my mom cried as she ran to hug him.

✺ 16 ✺

ZAMIR

Everybody's reaction was what I expected it to be. The whole backyard was decorated, and her garden was how she always kept it. I had a table set up in the middle with plates and menus, a cake table that had all kinds of treats, and lights that lit up the whole backyard. We had a small bar set up, and since Grandma's yard was so big, I had tikis around a square that I told them was the dance floor. I had a speaker playing music from my iPad and we would just go from there. We all sat down since dinner was first. We talked and smoked while the chefs brought out our dishes. Our appetizers were either boneless wings or shrimp Caesar salads. The main course was between rib eye steak or baked BBQ chicken breast, mac and cheese, cabbage, yams, mashed potatoes, gravy, greens, and yellow rice. My greedy ass had a little bit of it all and so did Justine.

"Baby, you did an amazing job," Denver told me as she ate some of the yams. The juice from them dropped down her lips and I couldn't help but lick it off. She smiled at me, and I got lost in her bedroom eyes. This girl was everything to me, even though I sometimes acted like she wasn't. I found myself admiring her dimples and the way the color white looked on her.

Her hair was done to perfection, as always, even though I had fucked it up before we left out the house. Her skin was glowing under the moonlight, and if I had a ring, I would ask her ass to marry me.

"Aight now, stop looking at my daughter like you 'bout to pounce on her at this damn table. You my son, so I don't want to have to have to beat yo' ass at this nice event you threw for Moms," Maurice said with a hint of laughter in his voice.

"Stop hating. I remember your ass used to look at me just like that," Trish gushed.

"Man, shut yo' ass up." He laughed.

I looked away from Denver and over at Justine, who had a look of sadness on her face. I was sure it was one or two things. Manny being all over his girl, or that everyone was here with someone, and she was alone. Which was why I told Denver not to invite her, but she insisted she come because she wanted to use that time to make amends and, in her eyes, she was family since she was carrying her nephew.

"Let me talk to you," Denver told Justine, and they both got up and walked over to the garden where Grandma had two chairs. I watched and ate while they talked. It looked like they both ended up crying and hugging. I didn't care what they said to each other, long as Denver came back over here happy. When they walked back over, everyone was clapping for them. I knew how much Denver was hurt by not being able to find her and things like that, so I was genuinely happy they were able to work out that problem. Despite Denver being mean, she was caring and loved hard.

"So, I did this tonight because I wanted to celebrate Grandma. We haven't been by this house in a while, and if we do come by, nobody comes in. I want to say that for her, we should at least come in and keep the garden up. We all know how she felt about her space. I've been grateful and thankful for y'all family since I was a little kid, but Grandma did the most when it came to me. There were times when I didn't know where my next meal would come from, and she would bring me right in here to eat. After the first time, she told me it would always be a plate here for me when I need it, as well as a bed and a hot shower. She may not have been my blood, but she was my family. When y'all let me know she was gone while I was in jail, I couldn't eat or sleep for days. I knew that had I kept my hands to myself a few times I would have been here holding everybody up like y'all did me so many times. I just want to say that love is love, and when I say that y'all know what I mean. I love y'all and would not be here without y'all. We love you and miss you, Grams," I said, raising my glass. A nigga almost shed a tear, but I didn't let it fall. Everyone raised their glasses and tossed back whatever was in there.

We gave speeches and took shots until everybody went. Next thing you know, the music was more up to speed and everyone was dancing or smoking and talking, but the party was on. I knew Denver was having fun because her shoes came off a long time ago.

"You're the best, you know that." Denver wrapped her arms around me.

"I heard you say something like that before, but I thought you was only saying that 'cause I was giving you this big dick," I joked, and she playfully pushed me.

I pulled the bracelet out my pocket and placed it on her wrist. She looked at it, and her eyes filled with tears that she quickly wiped away.

"You didn't," she cried.

"I did. The next jewelry I give you is going to come with me being on one knee. I needed you to have something that reminds you of them every day. They were the closest people to you and on this day, you deserve something to not remind you of the way you found Grandma but the way she loved you. Once you came around, the title for her favorite wasn't even debatable anymore. I love you and I'm tired of playing games with you. I'm not even asking you to be my girl because you are already that. You my lady, and I'm willing to die behind you. It's always been that way, but now it's official. It's us forever, and I promise one day soon, we gone walk down an aisle and I'm gone give you my last name and my kids." I held on to Denver.

"I love you too, and I can't wait for that day." She kissed me. The kiss we shared was as if no one else was in the room. My hands rested on her ass as we tongued each other down in the middle of the backyard.

"Okayyy," Sydney called out, making us pull apart. Denver wiped her lip gloss from my lip and went to walk away, but I pulled her back to me.

"Were yo' ass going?" I asked her while rubbing on her butt. I really pulled her back because my dick was hard, and I needed her to cover him until he went down.

"To show off my damn bracelet. You ain't slick either." She laughed.

"Roll up," I told her, handing her the weed and backwoods off the table. I sat down in the chair, and she was standing in between my legs with her back facing me. Since her shirt exposed her lower back and everyone was a little distance away dancing, I took my tongue and traced the line of her pants. Denver's back arched and she hissed. My hands rested on the back of her thighs while I licked up and down her back. Eventually, she passed me the weed and sat down on my lap.

"Why are you playing?" she asked as I blew smoke in her face.

"You the one who had that ass in my face. It's already big as fuck and I love eating it, so what was I supposed to do?" I questioned her, taking another pull before handing it back.

She sucked her teeth before taking a pull of her own. Denver placed her lips on mine and blew the smoke in my mouth before slipping her tongue into my mouth. One of my arms rested on her waist while the other slid up her shirt and caressed her breast. I rubbed one of her nipples through her bra, making her rock her hips in my lap. To others it may have looked like she was just facing me while she danced on me. I pulled away from her and looked up at her. Her eyes were still closed, so I kissed on her neck, leaving a mark like we were kids. She continued to smoke while I sucked and licked all over her neck, only stopping when she passed me the weed.

"I want some dick in the car," she told me bluntly.

"Whatever you want, baby," I agreed with her.

She slid her hands in my jeans and rubbed my dick, making my eyes close. My shit was on brick, so her hand felt good as hell. And since she was sitting on my legs, she had enough space to pull my shit out. Her thick thighs and the tablecloth covered what she was doing.

"You gone bust right fast?" she whispered.

I let the smoke out my mouth and licked my lips. With low eyes, I nodded my head at her. She let some spit fall from her mouth on her hand and my dick and jerked my shit. I had to lean my head on her shoulder while she choked my shit like a chicken.

"Za, you okay?" Trish asked me, and I nodded my head, not wanting to lift it up. Denver's nasty ass kept on stroking my shit too.

"You know I'm here if you need to talk, right? Don't be shutting down on us again." She kept talking.

"Fuck, I'm not trying to," I said a little too loud as I came in Denver's hand.

"Okay. You are fucking nasty," she told Denver as she walked off with a look of disgust.

Denver laughed while grabbing napkins. She wiped her hand while I wiped my dick and placed him back in my pants. She got up to go wash her hands while I rolled up. I sat there watching everybody mingle. Justine even looked like she was finally loosening up and having fun. Her belly was big now and she kept rubbing it. I even caught Manny going over to her a few times and rubbing her belly. She would just stop and let him do what he wanted for a second and when he walked away, she would let her eyes travel after him for a second. Then she would get back to whatever she was doing.

"You can tell that girl regrets everything she's done to him. You can also see that he ain't battling with himself over if he's making the right decision as far as her anymore," Maurice sat down and spoke.

"Yeah, I see. I'm still fucked up as to how she had all y'all dishing out money. I don't bring it up, though, 'cause my boy was really fucked up about it. I almost wished she ain't do that shit just off how she looks at him and how he is over her. I know he over her, but only time will tell if he's fully over her. Like right now, she's not seeing anybody, and he has cameras in her house. How he really feels will come out when she only allows him access to the footage in the baby room and she gets her a man," I spoke honestly.

My brother was my brother, right or wrong, and I wanted the best for him. Whatever or whoever he decided to be with, I wouldn't treat them funny or insert myself in their problems. I liked both girls for him, and I could see that Sydney was growing on him. I also liked how Justine didn't make a fuss out of things. She accepted shit for what it was. Denver's ass would have probably tried to kill me and the person I brought.

"So, you and Denver finally, huh?" He nodded her way as she came toward us with a big smile on her face.

"Yeah, but y'all been knew that. That's my baby, and I ain't letting shit get in between us," I said, and meant every word.

✻ 17 ✻

JUSTINE

TWO MONTHS LATER

I swallowed the huge lump in my throat. This man had a way of making me feel things I never felt before. However, he no longer belonged to me. I had the results to the DNA test he was so mad about taking. Manny had a fit every day about it but finally gave in last week and took the test. Now here he was again, throwing another fit about me not opening the paper.

"Come on, open the shit, you wanted to know so bad." He paced the floor.

"Emmanuel, I need my fucking key back, and you need to go home and open ya own fucking paper at your own time. My god damn feet are hurting, and I want to sit down and relax. I'll open mine when I feel like it," I shouted at him as I slid my slides off my feet and went and sat on the couch. I was eight months pregnant, and my feet were always swollen. Braxton-Hicks became a daily part of my life, and I was over this pregnancy. I didn't want a baby shower, for the simple reason of who was I going to invite? I did do a maternity shoot that I loved so much that I had one of the pictures blown up and hanging in my living room.

"Why you got to make shit so difficult all the time?" he asked.

"And how did I do that? You received the paper and drove your ass all the way over here to try and make me open the paper because you must be scared or don't want to see it alone. You could have easily done it with someone you are comfortable with." I sighed.

"It's only right we do it together," he whined like a damn baby.

"You could have called me on the phone," I spoke.

Just because he was getting on my nerves, and I wanted him to leave so I could get ready for work the next day, I ripped the paper open. My hand flew to my mouth when I saw the results.

"What? Say something," he called out to me.

Tears filled my eyes as I went to speak. However, Emmanuel snatched the paper from my hand and looked at the paper. He dropped to his knees and hugged me.

"I knew he was mine," he cried. Like, this man was literally shedding real tears. I wrapped my arms around him as he cried into my stomach.

"Daddy got you, lil' man, I promise." He kissed my stomach, and this little boy got to kicking and whatever else he was doing.

"Thank you for giving me my son, yo. I'm gone let up off you a little. I know I been getting on your nerves and stressing you out. My intentions are good though. We going to be co-parenting and I want it to go as smooth as possible. I'll keep him while you at work and meet you here with him or you can come pick him up from me. We gone make this work. I want you to find somebody that makes you happy and gone treat my son right. I was selfish at first for snapping on you and trying to dictate your life," he admitted, and I nodded my head.

"Thank you, Manny, for giving me something to love and someone to make proud. I'm not going to make your life hard either," I said and then got up. He was holding me for too long and my pussy was throbbing.

"Get yo' hot ass on. I can't cheat on my girl." He laughed.

"I'd never ask you to," I threw over my shoulder and went to take a shower to calm myself. I was over my baby daddy in a way. The only problem was being as though I was pregnant, my hormones were through the roof. I stepped into the bathroom and a contraction hit me. This one was completely different than the ones I had been feeling.

"Manny," I called out to him in pain.

Of course, he came running to me. I was bent over holding my stomach. The liquid gushing down my leg let me know my son was trying to make his entrance in the world, and it was way too early for that. Manny picked me up and carefully ran me outside to his car. He placed me in the backseat and hopped in the front before he took off.

"Please drive carefully," I cried out to him. That man ain't give a shit about what I was saying as he sped through traffic. Each time I screamed, he stopped the car to check on me. By the time we made it to the hospital, I was seven centimeters dilated and getting medicine was out the window. The pain I was in was bad, and each contraction felt like I had to take a shit, but it wouldn't come out. You know like the one where it feels like you are about to push your soul out your body and only a little turd comes out.

"Khasai is on his way," Manny said to someone on the phone as they rushed me to labor and delivery. They propped my legs up and Manny's dumb ass got to screaming. I swear I wanted to put him out.

"That's his head? My son ain't waiting on y'all to get ready, come on, son. Come on out, ya pops right here waiting." Manny was on his knees in front of me with his hands out.

"Excuse us, Dad, we have your son to deliver. I'm sure you said she was only eight months. We have to make sure he's okay and nothing's wrong since he is early. On three, I want you to push, and when I say stop, you stop. Remember to breathe," the doctor said and got in front of me. Manny came next to my head and helped me out.

"One, two, three." I began to push so hard I had to scream.

"Breathe, don't forget to breathe," the doctor told me after several pushes.

His head was right there, but his ass wasn't trying to come out. After my tenth push, I heard his cry and watched them as they carried my baby over to a station and did whatever they had to do.

"We're going to take him to the NICU. He's going to be placed in an incubator and under a heating lamp just for a short period of time to make sure he can keep his body temperature stable. I also want to give him an antibiotic shot to keep him from getting any infections. I'll have a nurse come down and talk to you about the NICU and everything I just said so you are aware of what's going on. Once you're cleaned up and given some medicine, they can bring you up and you can see the baby. He's three pounds and fourteen ounces, so we will also be keeping him until he's at least five pounds. Once you go up to the NICU, they will explain how they work, and you will meet his nurses," the doctor said before congratulating us and walking out.

"Was he tiny? Did he have hair? Was he light like you or dark like me?" I asked Manny since he was able to see him for a second and I didn't.

"He looked like a baby to me. He did have some hair, it was like slick, and I don't know what color he was. He looks like he has some kind of shit on him," Manny said.

"Where are you going?" I asked him when he got close to the door.

"Upstairs with my son. They are taking too long to clean you up. Call my phone when my mom and them get here or you done so I can bring you up. I miss my little nigga already," he said as he walked out.

I was a little jealous in the moment. I had waited eight long months to meet my boy and people were meeting him before me. I was glad I didn't have to get stitches and my lady parts no longer felt like they was on fire. After what felt like forever of being in the room alone, Trish and Maurice walked in.

"How is he? I know it's a little early for him to be born, and what do you want to do about testing? I have to ask you this now because we know when Manny gets back, he would flip about me asking you that." Trish sat down on the bed and rubbed my head.

"We don't have to do that. Manny and I did the test last week and he is Khasai's father," I replied, calling my son the name Manny picked.

"Okay, that's great. Now when can I see my grandbaby? And I want you to know we don't ever have to speak on the past, that's in the past. I want you to feel like family. My grandson can have whatever, just let me know," Maurice said.

I nodded my head just as Denver and Zamir walked in. Zamir was just as hype as Manny to have his godson in the world. He kept yelling how he was gone be the best god-dad in the world, and Denver had to ask if she could be his god-mom, since it would only be fair she got an extra title as well. Of course, I agreed.

"He's in NICU since he came early. Manny is up there, you guys can call him. Since I didn't get any medicine during birth, I'm about to take some now," I said, pointing to the tray that held my pill and juice. The nurse waited for me to take it before she left out, leaving me alone with these loud ass people. All I wanted to do was see my baby, take a nap, wake up, and tell my son I love him.

Manny came back into the room and took them two at a time to see Khasai while my ass impatiently waited. Visiting hours were ending soon, so I let everyone go before he wheeled me up there. My palms were sweaty, and my nerves were getting the best of me the closer we got. Manny stopped me in front of an incubator, and my baby was laying in there sleep. His name was on a little football with a little message underneath it. My baby boy was in a little pamper and a shirt and hat.

"Is it okay if we give him a binky? And do you want to hold him? If so, you're going to do skin to skin." The nurse smiled after introducing herself as Katie.

"Yes, I want to hold him. He's so tiny, oh my god. You sure it's okay if he comes out of there, and what are all those things hooked up to him?" I replied while she took her time taking him out after unhooking his cords. She placed him inside my gown on my chest and then hooked the cords back up.

"It's one for his oxygen levels, his heartbeat, and temperature. Yes, it's okay for you to hold him. Some babies come early and their skin is still soft, so that's the main time we don't let parents hold their babies, but that's not the case for him. I'll be going over his treatment plan with you and what we will need to see him improving in for him to go home. He's allowed four people on his visitor list besides you guys that you trust to come up here, or if you can't pick him up one of them will be able to. These are procedures we have to take, being as though people start having too many people up here and it causes problems." The nurse sat down and explained everything to us. I listened carefully to everything she said. When she was done, she got up and left, leaving us time with my son. I kissed his tiny fingers.

"I love you, Khasai. I promise to be the best mommy ever," I whispered to him. For the first time, I felt myself loving a person with everything in me. I was willing to give my life for his already, and I just met him.

❧ 18 ❧

ZAMIR

Mikey had called me and asked me to come over. I felt like a fucked-up cousin because it had been a while since I checked in on him or even found out what was going on with him. Most times I would drop off money and keep on going. I wasn't too worried about anybody bothering him or him getting himself in trouble because his ass still didn't get out much. He was sitting on the porch smoking a cigarette, which was new to me. His hair was a mess and it looked like he wasn't himself.

"What's going on with you, and when you pick up that habit?" I smacked the cigarette out his hand.

He may have been my big cousin, but I would knock his ass out before I let him finish that cigarette in front of me. I knew life was beating him up because he hated smoking anything. He hated addiction to things even more. One thing he always said was he wanted to help people get away from their addictions. He couldn't do that if he was addicted to something. Of course, he was talking about drugs, because that boy was damn sure addicted to his game.

"Trichelle left me," he whimpered.

I was expecting something totally different, yet I knew that hurt him. He and that girl been together for years, so her leaving had to be a buildup of some shit, because I knew he wasn't cheating. I sat there quietly and listened to him vent about how she wanted to go on dates, hang with her friends, and just enjoy life. He told me how she felt like he was holding her back and she wanted to live life like a normal person, not closed in a room all the time. And honestly, I couldn't blame her. This was the most I saw him outside since we were kids, and even then, he barely wanted to be out. He didn't like germs, and he didn't like crowds. My cousin would flip if he had to go to an event or be in a crowded place.

"Can you blame her? Not everybody wants to be caged in all the time. Shit feels like jail."

"You sound just like her," he growled.

"I mean, it's true. If you wanted your relationship to work, you were gone have to be willing to compromise. Take her on a few dates, you won't die. Either you want your girl, or you don't. You out here down bad. In fact, come on, we're going out in the streets. I'm gone get you right together."

I talked to him for about an hour more before I took him to the barber shop to get his hair cut and to the mall to grab him a few outfits. I was going to take him to the club, but the car waiting in front of one of our trap houses that I rode by had me changing plans. I dropped Mikey off back home and spun the block to make sure he was safely inside. I drove back to the trap house and parked up the street. Just like I was watching, so were the people sitting on the porch. Climbing out of the car with my hand in my gun, I walked up on the car. The window rolled down, and I saw Dice. He used to work for Kilo back in the day with me. We were never cool, but we never had problems either.

"Your people are moving on my blocks without my permission. I figure I come watch and see who was running this shit. Man to man, if you don't want shit to get ugly, you will keep them off my blocks," Dice stated rather calmly.

"I ain't moving shit, you know who the fuck I am. Now if you would have come over here with some positive shit for us to both make money, and come to an understanding, we could have talked like grown men. Yet, you on some bullshit, knowing I'd put your ass to sleep. Talking about your permission. These blocks open and you have people on one end that's barely out there. Your spot is more of the Papi store, and nobody from my camp comes over there," I said with the same tone of voice, even though inside I was burning up.

This man really had the nerve to be watching my people like he was going to do something. See, if he was me, his ass would have done something. I'm not letting nobody take my block or even set up on my shit. We would have worked something out from the get-go, but he wasn't on that. We had been set up on that block and working for weeks. His ass was just mad that our drugs were better. He climbed his big, slow ass out the car and pointed his finger my way.

"Listen here, boy, I been doing this shit a long time, and I'm not about to play with you. You and Manny can move your peoples, or we gone have a real got damn problem, you understand me." He got hyped up.

I laughed in his face. I wasn't doing shit, he was gone have to make us. We had guns just like they did, and they bled just like we did. Quite frankly, I was tired of being the bigger person in situations. He wanted to get tough for no reason. His ass came looking for us, we ain't come looking for him. Competition was at an all-time high right now, and we just so happened to be taking all the money and people couldn't stand that. I was never one to back down and I wasn't going to start now. This man walked up on me, and that was all she wrote. I took a step back and tried to avoid what I knew was to come. I hadn't put a nigga to sleep in a while, and here his old big ass was asking for me to take him to dream world.

"What the fuck you want to do, young blood?" his deep, raspy voice challenged me.

"Man, what the fuck you trying to do? Fuck is you talking

about? I'm on whatever you on. Pussy, you came at me. Now I done stepped back once and that was the only time. Walk up on me again and I'm gone lay yo' ass out," I threatened.

He threw his toothpick down, pulled his jeans up, and walked up swinging. He caught me once and that was all. I two pieced his ass so fast his legs gave out. His body locked up and his head bounced off the ground. All that and now his ass was on the curb sleep. His boys ran over, and we got to going. It was four of them on me and it quickly ended up being three as another went down. My guys must have peeped what was going on, because they ran over and started swinging too. We didn't stop until I was good and tired, and even then I let them go for a little longer before I called my guys off. Once they all stepped back, we waited to clutch our guns to see what they were gone do. They picked Fat Ass and his sleeping partner up and carried them over to their car. I laughed at their struggle.

"Man, this straight bullshit. He pissed off 'cause his shit overly stepped on and his team chill more than they trap out here. I told y'all that nigga was gone come with some problems. Aye, boss man, why you sleep him like that?" Gotti, one of our young workers, laughed.

"He came looking for trouble. One thing I don't want y'all to do is go searching for trouble, but if it comes your way, handle it the way you see fit. You don't always got to pull your gun, but don't let them pull out on you first either. You see a nigga clutch or reach, y'all better bust his ass first. I don't want to bury none of y'all, but I feel like some shit is brewing. We need to be more prepared. I'm gone have more people out here. They just gone be for backup and y'all ain't gone see them for that reason alone. If some shit goes down, I don't want y'all outnumbered. Don't hesitate, and it ain't no time to be scared. I see fighting or falling shit out as a way of finding a solution, but niggas like him is straight punks, and he ain't gone just take that. I put his ass to sleep like that in front of his peoples. Watch y'all ass out here and if y'all need me, call me. I'll be coming round here more too. We ain't ducking shit," I scolded them like they were my kids.

They all nodded, and I hung around for a bit longer just to see what was going to happen for the day. Even though I knew more than likely he wouldn't come back today, I still stayed outside. Manny was handling shit with his son, so I would put him up on game when I saw him. I refused to have him leave the hospital for some nut shit; however, he needed to know so that he could watch himself. I headed home and Denver's ass was in the kitchen with her bonnet on, some boy shorts that her ass swallowed, and a sports bra, cooking something that had my stomach growling.

I walked up behind her and wrapped my arms around her waist. "What's good, baby," I spoke, kissing her neck.

"Hey, how was your day?" she asked, not turning around.

"It was a regular day." I didn't even have to peek over her shoulder since I could see over her head. In the pot was yellow rice, pepper steak, and broccoli.

I backed up and bent down, kissing from her ass up to the back of her neck. Denver's head went back and her back arched. She let me kiss all over her before she turned around to face me. She frowned when she saw my face, and I already knew she was about to flip the fuck out.

"What the fuck? Who touched you, baby? Did you knock they ass the fuck out? Where they at? You want to go back? We can fuck them up together. My brother know you got into some shit?" She shot question after question, never giving me the chance to answer the first one. I picked her ass up and sat her on top of the island.

"I'm good. I'm here, ain't I? And nah, he doesn't know, but I'm gone tell him in a minute. I want him to worry about my godson right now. When he leaves, I'll put him up on game. As far as you and your peoples, I just need y'all to watch yourselves. Keep your gun on you at all times. Niggas ain't feeling us, and our work too good. Have your girls strapped too when they pick up from over southwest." I kissed her lips and helped her down.

She didn't ask any more questions, she just went back to cooking while I went to go take a shower. Our money was growing and so was our name, so I knew it would come with some kind of trouble. I just ain't know it would come that fast. I could have easily had Maurice go and handle shit with Fat Ass, but he wasn't in the game no more and we didn't need him stepping back in. I was going to hit him up and see if what I was thinking about doing was the right thing. I was tired of being the ones who got hit first. I learned a long time ago to be the person apologizing and not the person being apologized to. I could already see the people had to think we was soft because we weren't just running around busting our guns. We weren't taught like that. We fought first and if you wanted to take it to gun play, then by all means, we could take it there. Niggas was gone stop sleeping on us, and if I had to lay niggas down first, I would.

❦ 19 ❦

DENVER

My nephew was so cute, and I often found myself up at the hospital visiting him. I could go up whenever I wanted, and I would go around two in the morning. Sometimes Justine would be up there sleeping in the chair next to his bed or just sitting there. We would talk for a while, or I would read him books while she went and got herself together. The hardest part was when she was discharged, and he had to stay. That girl cried so hard. For the most part, she never left him alone. She stayed by his bedside unless one of us came up, then she would go home to shower. Other than that, she stayed glued to his side. Manny was just as bad, he didn't miss a day with his son. He wasn't there as much as Justine was, but he made it his business to see him every morning and night.

"I need one night with you home. Khasai will come home soon, and our asses can sleep together at Manny or Justine's house. But tonight, I just want to hold you. Let me put a baby up in you so we can have one of our own," Zamir said, pulling me back on the bed. His ass was mad I was getting my work clothes out so I could leave and go see my little baby. He knew I would be back in the morning to shower and get ready for work.

"I know, but he just so stinking cute. Plus, I'm a better

godparent than you are already. Oh, and while we're talking, what's up with the shipments and pickups? My girls said shit been a little slower." I looked over at him.

"'Cause we been switching shit up. Being as though we are expanding, we are stepping on other people's toes and they not feeling that shit. You know how I feel about traffic in and out the same spot. People will start watching and trying to figure out the pattern. If you paid attention to your burner phone, you would know that. I moved most of the team into separate locations. Each of your girls will have a spot no front entrance at all either. I don't even want both girls going. Whoever picks up goes there and they can meet the person who's going to do the drop and bring the money to you. I'll also be putting one of my guys with the person who collects the money and bring it to you just so they're not alone." He rubbed my back.

"Okay, anything else?" I asked him.

"Yeah, come to bed ma. I miss the fuck out of you. We been apart all day." He pulled me on top of him.

"I missed you too a little bit." I lied. I did miss his ass. I got so used to being around or with him that when I went to work, I found myself on my phone checking in on him every few hours.

He didn't let me go, even though I tried to climb off of him. Zamir held me in his arms until I fell asleep.

My alarm buzzing woke me up, and Zamir was no longer in bed with me. Sitting up, I stretched and then went to handle my hygiene and saw Zamir's ass was in the shower. I peed, wiped myself, and flushed the toilet. When I was done washing my hands, I brushed my teeth and washed my face. Stripping out of my clothes, I climbed in the shower with Zamir, and he instantly wrapped his arms around me. I looked up at him and smiled. He was so much taller than me that even in heels, I only came to his chest. I couldn't believe we were finally together. I remembered when I used to dream of this day. Zamir smirked at me before he kissed my forehead. We washed each other up and got out. While drying off, Zamir looked like he heard something.

"Yo, turn that music off right fast," he said while grabbing his gun. I grabbed my phone, turned the music off, and grabbed my gun as well. "Stay right there. Anyone comes in this room besides me, start throwing that shit," he whispered. I watched as Zamir slowly made his way out the room, aiming his gun with precision. I stood with my back against the wall near the door so whoever came in would have to turn and see me. I waited for what seemed like forever, but the clock on the cable box let me know it had only been two minutes.

Tightening my towel, I kept my gun in my hand and jogged down the steps. Zamir's ass was in the backyard looking like a damn shooter in a movie the way he was hitting corners. Just as he went to come back in, I saw a guy with his hood on coming up over the neighbor's gate. I aimed my gun like my dad taught me to and let off a shot, hitting him in the forehead. It seemed like that one shot was the single cause for bullets to start flying. Zamir was hit once in the arm, and he dropped his gun and went to dive toward it. I shot in every direction I could before backing up into the house. Next to the back door was a shotgun. I grabbed it and cocked that bitch. I was gone blow a hole in somebody. I shot that bitch once and almost flew back inside of the house. I got my feet together and let off another shot, and it did exactly what I wanted it to do. Send them big niggas running. Once I was sure nobody else was gone shoot, I ran over to Zamir. Blood was coming from his mouth and his eyes were closed. I knew damn well he wasn't dying on me. I grabbed the guns we both used and ran back in the house and placed them in the safe we had built in the ceiling. While hiding everything, I dialed for help. I screamed to them that my boyfriend was shot and that we needed help. When they assured me not to move him and that help was on the way, I called my brother and father. This shit was like déjà vu to me, and I was starting to hate back yards.

I applied pressure to the wounds I did see and waited for help to come. The first people to arrive was the cops. I let out a small breath when I saw Sydney was the white shirt that came out. She did most of the searching and collecting of shell casings. She's also the one who took my statement, which was simple.

"We were in the shower and got out when we heard some noise. Zamir came down to check it out. I heard shots go off and I ran downstairs. I couldn't come out because it was people on both sides shooting. It looked as if they were shooting at each other. Zamir was caught in the middle. Once I got to him and saw he was shot, I called the police and tried to get help," I told part of the truth.

Only thing they could go by was my word, and that's what they would have to take for now. They asked if I wanted to go down to the station and I quickly declined. I wanted to be with Zamir and make sure he was okay.

"I called your brother. I'm sure he's on his way here. There's nothing in the house I should be concerned or try to steer away from, is it? I also noticed guns in your house. They're all registered, right? I'm going to need your license to carry if you have one, just so they don't try and take you down for them," Sydney said.

She had me pulled to the side with her notepad out like she was getting information. Once she said it was okay for me to go, I ran out the front door straight into Manny's chest. He grabbed me so I wouldn't fall. When I saw my brother, I broke down crying.

"Where my brother?" he asked me.

I tried to get it out, but nothing came out. I pointed toward the ambulance truck and Manny ran over to it. He tried to pull the door open, but it didn't budge. He began banging on the door, causing the medics to pull off. We jumped in his car and followed close behind them with the cops close behind us.

Manny didn't stop until we got to the hospital, and when they pulled Zamir out the back, he flipped his shit. He was yelling at me, asking me what happened, why, and how. As always, he tore some shit up in the waiting room and was about to get put out.

"If he doesn't calm down, we are going to have to ask him to leave. He's tearing things up and being excessively loud," the lady from the front desk came and told me.

"Who gone put me out? Ain't nobody gone fucking touch me. Now you can come over here and say all that, but can't tell me shit 'bout my god damn brother. Bitch, take dick up your ass dry and love it before you come over here with that bullshit again," he spat.

I looked at the nurse with a sorry expression. Wasn't nothing I could do to stop her. Trish walked in along with my aunty Niecy, who I hadn't seen since her ass got her a new man and started traveling the world on his dime. Aunty Niecy pulled me into a long hug while Trish went and got a hold of her son.

"Y'all father on his way," she told us as she held onto Manny, who broke down like he was a baby. Trish held onto him and rubbed his head while he let out a gut-wrenching cry that made us all shed a tear of our own.

"How many times was he hit?" Trish asked.

"I only saw the one on his arm. It was so much blood I didn't even know where to apply pressure to. I just tried to keep his head turned because he had blood coming from his mouth. I tried to help him, it just was so many people. All they kept screaming was ain't nobody just gone move on the block without war. I swear God ain't letting up on me. We were just fine, talking about kids and businesses. Now look, he's hurt. I should be back there with him. He's always taking up for me, helping me, and protecting me. I haven't done that for him yet. I tried so hard to, though, and it just didn't work out like that," I cried.

Aunty Niecy let me know that everything was going to be alright, and I wished I believed her. Zamir didn't deserve any of this, none of us did. We sold drugs and made money. We weren't out here just starting unnecessary drama or wars. We minded our business, and yeah, we were expanding on blocks, but they weren't claimed. It wasn't like we had stolen territory. You worked on whatever block you wanted. The only time we didn't was if someone told us that's where they been trapping. I felt like Zamir getting shot was another sign for me to give all this shit up. I didn't want to lose my family or my own life over a block or some drugs. Hell, the only drug I did was weed, and that couldn't kill me. The doctor was taking forever to come out and the more I waited, the sicker I felt to my stomach. My dad showed up and was acting almost as bad as his son. I felt myself explaining what happened over and over, and I was growing tired of it. Manny had left for a while and came back. When the doctor finally came out, we all damn near ran to him.

I didn't even know what he said because I had gone into a panic attack the moment I saw all the blood on him. I got to screaming and visions of Zamir's body falling flooded my mind. Someone held on to me and I didn't even know who.

"Why, please, I need him to be okay," I cried out.

❧ 20 ❧

MANNY

Since my son was born early, I spent each day at the hospital in the NICU with him. Overall, he was healthy, they just wanted him to gain weight and he could come home. He had no problem latching into his mom's nipple nor the bottle. She had said she wanted him on both breast milk and formula, and since I didn't know shit, I didn't disagree. Khasai came in this world weighing three pounds and fourteen ounces. He didn't have his looks yet, so I couldn't say who he would look like. His brown skin was a shade darker than mine and to me, he was perfect. He would often suck his fingers, and his doctor said it was a sign he was hungry. I was happy as hell and felt like life was finally moving forward for me. Sydney didn't complain once about the amount of time I was spending at the hospital. With each day that passed, I understood that she was it for me. I was also spending a lot of time at Justine's house getting my son's room together while she was resting or up at the hospital, probably getting on the people's nerves.

Sydney pulled a lot of strings for me and got a few officers on my payroll that used to work with her dad. Of course, I didn't have that many because I wasn't making that much money. I had enough to where I wasn't worried, but I wasn't filthy rich yet. My dad was even starting to help out some with the businesses. I could tell he wanted to get his hands dirty when it came down to the Blu situation, but I wouldn't let him. I had a crew following Blu and was going to watch his every move. I was having fun with him for now because he felt like he couldn't be touched. I had paid a few females I knew from the hood that were in jail and were never coming home to pay his mom a visit, and I was just waiting on the call to say it was done. All the while, I was waiting for a chance to get at him.

See, what he didn't pay attention to was not only did I have people following him, but there was someone else following him too. I also wanted to have the drop on the person and know who they were. I wasn't trying to lose anyone doing footwork for me. Sooner than later, he was going to have to see me. My son coming pushed everything back. At first, I wanted everything handled and all beef squared away before my son's arrival. However, Khasai's ass wanted to make an early appearance and fucked my plans up. I was happy my boy was here and overall healthy. I was also glad that he was getting the help he needed and was growing little by little every day. Each test they gave him, he passed, and I just knew he would.

My phone rang for the second time, breaking me out my thoughts. I sat the piece to his swing down before I finally answered it.

"Yo," I answered the phone.

"It's been a shooting at your sister's house," was all Sydney told me before she hung up.

I was pretty sure she was working because had she not been, Sydney would have given me more details and wouldn't have hung up on me.

Dropping everything and jumping up off of the floor, I ran out the house and jumped in my car. I raced to my sister's house. Zamir had already warned me the last time I talked to him about Dice and their fight, so I had a clue who did the shit. My heart felt like it was about to beat out my chest. My boy had better be good, or I was going to show people that we weren't taking no more L's. When I made it there and saw my sister covered in blood, my mind went blank. Running over to the ambulance, I tried to rip the fucking door off to make sure my boy was good. When they pulled off instead of the door opening, the only thing we could do was follow them. Denver gave me the run down on what happened while I was driving, and my anger grew. Our houses were too accessible, and I was starting to see why my parents moved out the hood. It was no way any of us was going to stay where we were. 'Specially not while I had my son who would be frequently visiting everyone's home.

The fact we had to keep moving wasn't sitting too well with me. I felt like niggas were making us run.

When we got to the hospital the wait was so long, I started flipping out. My mom hugging me only helped for a second. When she let me go, I didn't care about what the doctors had to say. Deep down, I knew my boy wasn't going out like that, not yet. I called up the team of shooters on my burner phone and told them to meet me. Dice wanted to pull up on people and now I was going to return the favor. I was sure he and his team were acting like they had one up on us, and I was also sure they didn't think we would come back tonight, but we were. Once we all were at the warehouse, I handed out guns. Wasn't nobody going in with anything small either. We had Dracos, ARs and all kinds of big shit. I wanted to get in and get out fast so I could make my way back to the hospital like I never left. I would even go see my son just to make sure he was cool when I was done.

"We are going in, doing what we got to do, and we are leaving. Nobody gets left behind and protect whoever you nearby. Everybody watches everybody's back, that's how we will ensure we all make it back safely. That's the plan. Don't drive crazy and risk us being pulled over. I want everybody in there dead. Say y'all prayers too, God got us," I told them while they suited up.

Every time I did something I knew I shouldn't, I prayed about it beforehand.

We strapped up and walked out the door. I had on my bullet-proof vest and was ready to kill. We all piled up in cars and made our way through the city to Dice's trap house. The block was quiet, but that was only for now. We spun the block three times just to be on the safe side. I had a person watching each corner for the cops. I was doing my best to make sure all our asses were covered. I was used to going on missions like this with just Za, now we had a whole team, and I was going to use them to my advantage. Just as I expected, no one was outside, but walking up and climbing the back gate, you could hear niggas loud and clear celebrating. I wanted Dice's head and I was aiming for him first. Raising my foot, I kicked the back door down and started busting my gun from there. Bullets riddled through the kitchen. We had niggas shooting from so many angles, I was surprised we didn't shoot each other. None of them had a chance to duck or react.

"What the fuck, man," I heard Dice yell. Using my scope, I searched the room for his fat ass. He was using another nigga as his shield. I put the beam on his head and tapped the trigger, sending shots into his head. Once his body dropped, I backed out the door.

"Let's go," I called out.

We all took off running to our cars and pulled off. For the first time in my life, no one on my team was hurt and we all made it back in one piece. We got rid of the guns we used, and I pulled off my all black and was back in the clothes I came in.

"Y'all be safe." I slapped hands with everyone and let whoever wanted off for the night go be with their family, and whoever wanted to trap went back to trap. I went back to the hospital and read a book to my son, said a prayer with him, and watched as he stirred in his sleep.

"Lord, forgive me for my sins," I whispered.

I wanted to be around for my son, which was why anybody who felt some type of way about me couldn't live. I was starting to see why people were shooting first and asking questions later.

I was no longer fighting. You wanted smoke and I was giving it. My son needed a father, and I'd be damned if he didn't have one. After sitting there for a while, Justine showed up. Her face was bare, and her hair was up in a bushy ponytail. I could tell by how thick it was that she had washed her hair and barely blow dried it out like she always did. I gave her a quick hug then allowed her the seat I was sitting in. She reached in Khasai's bed and rubbed the side of his face. One of the nurses came over and helped her get him out so she could hold him. They pulled me another chair up and for a while, we both just watched him.

"Are you okay? I can see it on your face something is wrong," Justine whispered like she would wake him up.

"Za got shot. He in the hospital. I just needed to come be with my son," I replied.

Justine's free hand went to her mouth and before she even asked was he okay, she let a few tears fall, which let me know she genuinely cared for my peoples. "He's okay, right?" she finally asked, and I shrugged my shoulders.

"I don't know. I'm going to head out in a second to go see. I'll be back though. You're staying here for tonight?" I asked, because she was getting comfortable in the big seat they got her. She would often fall asleep in that chair. So, each time she came, if no one was using it, the nurses would give it to her, especially at night. A few people stayed, but not a lot.

"Yeah, I can't go home without my baby." She kissed his small cheek.

Nodding my head, I kissed her forehead and walked out. Being with my son brought me a sense of peace, which was one of the many reasons I stayed up under him.

I made the drive to Presby Hospital and went inside the waiting room. Everyone was still sitting around just waiting, which was the exact reason I left in the first place. It must have been just my luck because when I sat down, the doctor came out. Before he could even get a word out, Denver took one look at his clothes and started screaming and crying. I knew just by the way she was breathing her ass was panicking and hyperventilating. My mom and aunt ran to her side and wrapped her up in their arms. She started asking "why" and saying all kinds of shit that I was trying to block out.

"Do you want me to get her some help?" the doctor asked, concerned.

"No, she will be fine. Just please inform us on what's going on with my son. We've been out here for hours with nothing to go off of," my dad said.

"Zamir is still in surgery, he was shot a total of seven times. We did remove a few bullets, some are seeming too risky right now. I came out to tell you guys that we are doing the best we can to save his life but as of right now, we can't call it."

✲ 21 ✲

JUSTINE

When Manny left out, I said a quick prayer for all of them. I prayed that Zamir made it and I prayed that no more harm came their way. I may not have been close with them how I would like, but they were still good to me and my son, family before anything. When my son did a little whine, I gave him his small bottle and watched as he chugged it down. When he finished, I began to pat his back and he let out a tiny burp. I laid him down and changed his pamper. Khasai sucked on his binky and fell asleep. I got comfortable in my chair and laid there looking at the ceiling. I wanted to go and see if Zamir was okay, but I also didn't want to leave my son alone. I called Manny twice and he didn't answer, so I sent him a text letting him know I was thinking of them and wondering if everyone was okay.

"You know I sit here with my son every night and just stare at you. You seem like you got the stress of the world on you," the guy next to me said. His son was here before mine, and he always was getting a lot of work done on him. I would often find myself checking on him when his machines would go off.

"Umm, I don't know what to say to that, honestly. I really just been trying to focus on my son and nothing else. Life wasn't always easy for me. I want to give my son better and all the love I can while I'm here," I replied, looking over at him.

I tried not to stare into his dreamy bedroom eyes but found myself doing so anyway. I felt so wrong admiring his chocolate-colored skin, light-brown eyes, and the deep waves that ran through his head. He was sporting a black T-shirt and black sweats. His shoe of choice was a pair of white and black Nike dunks. Even in lounge wear I could see how fit his body was. The way his shoulders filled the shirt, I could easily picture me holding on to them while he bounced me up and down on his tool. I shook my head, clearing my mind of all the nasty thoughts that flooded my mind.

"I haven't seen anyone else up here but you, why is that? If you don't mind me asking," I said, trying to keep the conversation going.

"His mom left him here. I don't know where she went or why she left, and it's been two months. My parents are in the process of buying a house here. They live in Florida, but they are coming back here to help me. I drive trucks for a living and for the most part, I try and take the trips that are closer to home so I can get back here to him. I hate that I be having to leave him sometimes for days at a time, but if I didn't, we wouldn't have any money. I took a lot of time off when he first was born. Now I trust the nurses, so I don't feel as bad leaving him here. The guy that just left, that's your man?" he asked me.

"No, he is my son's father though. We have a cool bond, that we still kind of have trouble with. He's a good guy, and I messed up what we did have. For a moment I regretted it, but now it's like I learned from it and am moving forward. He has a girl. I just want to make my son happy, and that would start with his father and I having a healthy thing going as far as co-parenting," I admitted.

"What's your name? I never got it, mine is Tyler, I'm twenty-six." He extended his hand.

"Justine, and I'm twenty-two." I shook his hand.

We sat there talking for hours. Tyler made me laugh throughout the night. We stayed up late talking about our kids and just life period. I was happy I had someone to talk to who didn't judge me and was nice. I didn't tell him my whole life story, but each question he asked me I answered honestly. One thing I wasn't trying to do was start any friendships with a lie.

"I have to get to work. I have a drop off that I have to make by tomorrow morning. I hope to see you when I get back, beautiful," Tyler said to me right after he kissed his son on the forehead. He turned to me, and I waved him goodbye. Manny was walking up and looked between us both. The smile was quickly wiped off my face when he did a double look. I didn't need him causing no scene at the hospital.

"How are you doing? I'm Tyler, I hope you don't mind me talking to Justine." Tyler extended his hand and Manny shook it.

"Nah, bro, you good, just surprised me that's all. Justine deserves to be happy and if you can do that, we are good," Manny said, taking me by surprise.

Tyler nodded his head before he left and went to work. Manny sat down after calling one of the nurses over. She helped him put Khasai in his shirt for their skin-to-skin moment.

"Okay, miss finding love at the hospital," he joked.

"Shut up. Where's your cop lady?" I shot back.

"Probably at work. We haven't been seeing too much of each other lately." He sighed.

"Well, fix it. Make time for her. I'm sure with everything going on you can use a moment with her. Plus, I texted you last night and you never told me how Za was doing," I replied to him.

"'Cause I don't know. Nothing changed really. He's no longer in surgery but he still ain't woke," he told me while feeding Khasai.

I looked at Manny for a second. I knew him well enough to

know he didn't want to talk about it. Standing up, I walked over and kissed him and my son on their heads, then went home to take a shower. I climbed in my bed and closed my eyes. Even though I couldn't sleep, it felt good to lay in my bed. I thought about Tyler and how his smile was so contagious. I wondered if he was going to use my number, or if he got it last night just because. I was very happy that he and Manny got off to a good start, so if he asked me out on a date we could go. Manny didn't control who I talked to, but I figured if they got along, it would make everything easier for me. I was working on my life going smooth. In my lifetime, I had enough drama to whereas I didn't want any more. I hoped whatever Tyler was going through with his child's mother, they figured it out, because if he pursued anything with me, I did not want to be arguing and fighting with her if she decided to pop back up.

Grabbing my phone, I sent Denver a nice long text making sure she was okay and letting her know that I would pray for them. Since having my son, I'd been turning to God a lot. I wasn't saying I was going to go to church, but I was going to find God and put him first in my life. I wanted to raise a good, God-fearing young man. I knew he was gone be that mixed with hood because every man in his life was hood as hell. They all were outstanding in their own way. A smile graced my face when my phone dinged and a message from Tyler came through. It was a simple "hope your day is going well" text, but it had my ass smiling like when you first hear I love you from someone.

I was overall happy that someone was thinking about me like I was thinking about them. I texted him back before getting snuggled up under my blankets. I knew Manny would call me when he was getting ready to leave, so I was able to relax without calling the nurses and bugging them. I closed my eyes for a brief second and woke up two hours later.

I looked at my phone and saw I had a few missed calls from Manny and Trish. I instantly panicked, thinking something was wrong with my son. I called Manny back first.

"Khasai okay? I fell asleep by accident. I'm about to be on my way up there now," I spoke into the phone.

"Yeah, he's straight. You don't have to go up there right now if you don't want. I was calling to tell you I was leaving. My mom and dad up there with him. They said they wanted to spend some time with him, and I figured your ass was sleep. You deserve to get some comfortable rest. Go up there after you take some you time. I'm gone send you some money, go get them naps done and relax, they got him," he assured me.

I thanked him before hanging up on his ass. I trusted his parents with my son, but that still didn't stop me from calling them on FaceTime so I could see him. When they told me I didn't need to come up there right away, I laid my head back down on the pillow. I didn't even care about going to get my hair done. All I wanted to do was enjoy the comforts of my bed. I responded to a few text messages before I dozed back off.

❧ 22 ❧

BLU

Death just kept missing me and I didn't know why. At this point, I was so paranoid I found my ass up in church or at my grandmother's house. I would rather deal with her and the house being on fire than out in the world and being killed.

The thought of Zamir being so close he could have blown my head off kept replaying in my head. The only thing that saved me was I was in my patrol car.

Grabbing my coffee, I placed it in the cup holder and pulled out of Dunkin Donuts drive-thru. Just as I went to turn out of the parking lot, tires screeching could be heard. I looked over and Zamir pulled up next to me. I knew it was him because I could see his eyes. He rolled the window down just enough for me to see the gun he was pointing at me. The green beam that shined off of it had to be on my head because I didn't see it anywhere in the car.

"One day soon, I'm gone blow your shit back. You lucky you in that patrol car or I would have followed your ass and sent you with your boy. I heard his ass just went missing." He laughed and pulled off.

That was three days ago, and my ass had been calling sick off of work and staying in the house. They asses waited all this time, and I knew now they were out to get me, and I didn't want to be caught. I was sleep deprived and jumping at the sound of everything. I was on the verge of getting rid of my cat because the bitch was scaring me. Every night she would roam the halls knocking into shit, and I would jump up and point my gun at the door waiting hours for somebody to come in, for it to never happen. I often had thoughts of just killing myself; however, each time I placed my gun to my head, I put it back down. I wasn't built to do no shit like that, and no matter how scared I was of what they would do to me, I was even more scared of shooting my own self and not dying.

My captain was even on my ass. My partner had gone missing, and I didn't show an ounce of concern. It wasn't that I wasn't concerned, I was more scared than anything. For one, I didn't know when it would be my turn, and for two, I didn't want them to find out his disappearance had something to do with me. I cried with his family on the news, but deep down inside, I was happy. My secrets and all that bad shit I had done on the task force couldn't come out anymore, and the only person that knew just how many rules I had broken as a cop and could expose me was gone, and I'm sure he wasn't just missing. His ass was dead, and all the searching they were doing was all for nothing. I grabbed a pair of jeans and a shirt and got my day started. I skipped my shower because I had an important meeting that I was already almost late to.

My mom's lawyer had called me earlier, waking me out of my sleep, and asked me to come and meet him. I hadn't talked to him since the very morning of her sentencing. She asked him to not tell me anything and let her talk to me. I waited on that call for a while, but it never came. Now here I was parked outside of his house, a nervous wreck.

My nerves were literally all over the place as he got inside of my car and instructed me to drive. He didn't give me a location to go to, he just told me to drive, and that's what I did. I sat quietly as he talked, reading off of notes.

"Your mom was found dead in her cell about a week ago. I've

been trying to get in contact with you since then. Her cause of death has yet to be determined. She did leave you with everything she had left. However, it wasn't much, a few thousand to be exact," he told me.

My car came to a screeching stop. My mom was gone, and nobody knew why. She was where she was in the first place because of me. Everything that was happening was because of me. I felt like I was suffocating as I tried to catch my breath while I cried.

"Look, man, you can't blame yourself too much for what's going on. Your mom made the decision to be there, not you. Try and take this one day at a time. Since we can't locate your father or which prison he is in, we need you to be the person who steps up and gives her a proper burial. I can do what I can to have the state release her body to you, and you can send her home how you see fit. Her insurance policy is no longer effective because the bill for that hadn't been paid in years. I'm sure you know why. Please don't let your mother down. She didn't do all that she did for you so you could be out here about to get yourself killed." He reached over and squeezed my shoulder.

I didn't give a damn what he was talking 'bout. I was still trying to accept the fact that my mom was gone. I never got a chance to tell her thank you or how sorry I was for putting her through everything I did. My mom wasn't perfect, but she never gave up on me. She never talked down on me, and she loved me through every mistake I made. She would keep my head up and tell me that things happen, and we weren't the mistakes we made. It's what we did to fix them, how we learned from them that made us the person we were. I wished like hell I could rewind time and do everything differently. My mom wouldn't have been in jail, and she damn sure wouldn't have died in there.

I dropped her lawyer back off at home and drove around with an empty mind. I grabbed the pint of Jack out of my glove compartment and took a nice long sip to calm myself down. My mother was dead, and I wouldn't be surprised if Manny was the reason behind it. I was sure he was sending me another message, and whether he knew it or not, they were all being received, and I was clear on the message behind it. I had violated by coming at their whole family, so he was returning the favor by getting everyone close to me so I could suffer before he came for me. I was on edge, and even though I was wishing I could have a redo on life or just a chance to do shit different and right my wrongs, it looked like that wasn't in God's plans and death was the only way to correct me. As I drove around, I thought of anywhere I could go to clear my head and sulk in the memories of my mother, good and bad. Yet, I felt like nowhere was safe. The one place I could still feel her at was her home, so I drove there. Pulling up to my parents' house, I was surprised to see a car in the driveway. I used my key to let myself in. Walking around the house, everything was the same as I last saw it, besides the bottle of half-empty Jack on the countertop. The basement door came flying open, and my dad came out. He had an evil glare on his face when he looked at me.

"You know my wife is dead and I finally feel completely empty inside. I only ever wanted to give her another child. One that didn't give her trouble all the damn time. You know she loved the hell out of you, despite all the crazy things you did, like killing her dog and her cat. She even covered for you when you started harming Dakotah. That's why she put you out. You snuck in and killed that little girl and left, leaving us to take the wrap for you. I lost my career, my wife, and my child. You fucked up my background in so many ways. When I found out I was coming home, I was pissed. All that I had left in my savings could have me surviving in jail, but out here, I would barely make it a few months. And what kind of job do you think I can get? Because I can't come up with one." He switched his tooth-pick from the left side of his mouth to the right.

"Dad, it's not my fault. I didn't mean to harm that little girl, she just reminded me so much of my cousin and you let him die. You hated him because he had Denver, and all along, you were in love with her mother. You never even been with the lady, but you loved the way she walked and flipped her hair. How she lived life without a care, and not to mention, she was messing with your worst enemy. You have me out here trying to kill these people. You're the one who told me she had my cousin killed because they got into a fight. You're the one who told me that Justine didn't love me, that no one would ever love me because I'm a fucked up individual, when all I ever really wanted to do was make you proud," I cried.

"You're full of shit. You blame everything on everyone but yourself, and you are right. I told you I wanted them all dead. Including your crazy ass grandma, which was why I started slipping her them crazy pills a long time ago, and now her ass really is bat-shit crazy. That entire family owes me. That's my daddy's funeral home, and inside those walls are millions of dollars in cash. Denver was the reason your cousin was killed. A guy saw him beat her ass one day and stepped in, and it started a beef between them that led to him being dead. Your grandmother never looked at me the same after that day. All because we weren't allowed to pick him up and place him in our car. I tried to bring him back, but it was too late." My dad pulled an old rusty gun from his waist that I wasn't even sure still worked. He aimed at me and fired, letting a shot rip through my stomach. I closed my eyes and asked God to forgive me for all that I'd done.

As pain kicked in full force and I accepted my fate, I had finally found the answer to why I was the way I was. My father was the sole reason behind most of the things I did. I wanted to be just like him and everything he did, I followed. I picked up his selfishness and the way he would harm anyone, including his family, just so things could be how he wanted. Even now, with me knowing I was knocking at death's door, I had evil thoughts and hoped his last days on Earth were worse than mine. I wanted his death to come slow and with torture, like some gruesome shit you would see on a movie or read in a book.

He let off a few more shots into my body. Opening my eyes

back up, I looked at my dad in shock. This was not how my life was supposed to end. I was supposed to close this chapter with some positive shit and start on a new one, making that shit my life. Instead, the last words I would ever hear were, "You should have done what I said, because now they have a new enemy they will never see coming."

Made in the USA
Coppell, TX
17 November 2021

65934284R00080